Praise for
Gray Area

"Unwavering and profoundly human, *Gray Area* pulls back the curtain on what it means to survive in the aftermath of a school tragedy. Leah Decker's razor-sharp narration delivers a raw, intimate portrait of trauma, ethics, and resilience without veering into melodrama. Ideal for readers of memoir-style fiction and emotional complexity, this debut leaves a lasting mark."

—Dr. Todd Brown,
US Congressional Teacher of the Year,
United Nations education ambassador

"Everyone who has survived—or even attempted or considered attempting—a teacher preparation program needs to read *Gray Area*. Throughout the novel, I found myself relating tremendously to Decker's protagonist, Rachel Harding. She made me laugh one moment and cry the next. At times I wanted to grab ahold of Rachel, shake sense into her, even yell at her. Then, a few pages later, I wanted to wrap her in a hug and comfort her. Decker beautifully captures the complexities and nuances of working in US schools in the twenty-first century."

—Shaila Walker, high school educator

"[Leah has] captured a beautiful, important story that should honestly be read by any educator or anyone who loves an educator. We all carry those kinds of moments with us, and Rachel captures the feelings attached to that trauma very well. Her voice is honest and raw, humanizing how we live both in and out of the classroom in the face of trauma. I found her to be genuinely relatable, especially as an introverted person."

—Erin Haney, high school educator

"Leah Decker's portrayal of an aspiring teacher is downright fascinating. One suspects from the first few pages that the author is speaking from personal experience about secondary school teaching, and this suspicion is confirmed throughout. The storyline, taking us through the final year of the college/student-teaching process, is engaging enough to keep the reader's interest to the end. But it is the word painting of Rachel, the main character, that is extraordinary. She is at once confident and laser-focused on a teaching career, but unsure of what else she wants from life. She is a bit fragile, for sure, but finds the will to navigate, and, in the end, she comes to know (and like) herself as well as we do. A warm and interesting read."

—William Waddell, author

Gray Area
by Leah Decker

© Copyright 2025 Leah Decker

ISBN 979-8-88824-858-4

All rights reserved. No part of this publication may be reproduced, stored in a retrieval system, or transmitted in any form or by any means—electronic, mechanical, photocopy, recording, or any other—except for brief quotations in printed reviews, without the prior written permission of the author.

This is a work of fiction. All the characters in this book are fictitious, and any resemblance to actual persons, living or dead, is purely coincidental. The names, incidents, dialogue, and opinions expressed are products of the author's imagination and are not to be construed as real.

Edited by Miranda Dillon
Cover design by Catherine Herold

Published by

3705 Shore Drive
Virginia Beach, VA 23455
800-435-4811
www.koehlerbooks.com

GRAY AREA

LEAH DECKER

VIRGINIA BEACH
CAPE CHARLES

For every educator who has held onto their softness.

"Do you understand the violence it took to become this gentle?"
—Nitya Prakash

PREFACE

*P**lease, for the love of God, don't let Charles pee his pants today.*

That's honestly all I was thinking that morning. Charles had a problem with wetting himself, and I really didn't need to deal with that today.

It was a quarter after eight, and the students would be making their way into the building any second. I knew this because I had just pushed my way through the crowd of them to the front door of the school. They didn't give me, a lowly student teacher, a key, but I needed to get in early to set up for the day.

It was my first day teaching a lesson.

Slithering through the crowd of twelve-year-olds, many of whom were taller than me, only to knock on the door of the school was humiliating. It was demoralizing. How was I supposed to garner any respect from the students if they saw me this way every morning? Getting pushed back and forth by their colorful backpacks, looking out for projectiles being thrown, the nice ones calling out "Good morning, Miss H!" while the mean ones gave me dirty looks for seemingly no reason. I had to think they were just hormonal.

That was the thing about middle schoolers: They are so childish but think they are so grown up. They looked like children, but many of them swore and glared like adults. Some of them, of course, still acted very much like kids. Like Charles, who had a problem with his bathroom needs. And always first thing in the morning.

I always thought that Charles was much too formal a name for a boy that acted like such a baby. Someone named Charles should be an old-money upper-crust man in the North East. This kid I had to walk down to the office for fresh pants could at least be a Charlie or a Chuck. But no, for some reason this kid chose to go by his formal full name, Charles. And some days Charles was the bane of my existence.

He sat in the back corner of the classroom, by himself, as designated by the seating chart his first-period social studies teacher created. She was the kind of old-school teacher who took the problem kids and shoved them to the back. Out of sight, out of mind. This kind of thinking was highly discouraged by my New Age liberal arts college teacher preparation program. We only read the newest and most left-leaning literature about how to make students as apt to learn as possible. As if any of it could make a difference with these kids.

Looking back now, I can imagine little Charles with his buckteeth and his perpetually wet pants at 8:30 a.m. I remember him before, how he seemed like such an arrogant little kid who got his kicks by making adults like me regret my career path. I remember myself before: so sure, so black-and-white.

I remember Charles after everything, how I looked at him with my new eyes of empathy and wished that more than anything I could take his hurt away. Take all their pain away. Before, I was wondering when Charles was going to grow up and stop acting so childish. After, I was wishing that Charles could have stayed an innocent child forever.

CHAPTER ONE

I ALWAYS WISHED THAT I had just one ounce of nepotism in my life. That my parents or really anyone in my family could have had some connection to someone in power who could help me acquire a brilliant job in some fantastic field. Or at the very least that could have helped me get a better student-teaching placement.

When you're studying to become a secondary education teacher, you have to spend some time essentially interning underneath an experienced teacher in order to get hands-on experience working with students. Elementary teachers didn't have to begin their student teaching until after winter break, but secondary teachers-in-training like me had to begin almost immediately in order to get enough hours in by the end of the school year. Apparently, the program heads at the University of Big Bend thought that the experience needed with middle or high schoolers was greater than that needed to work with young children. But maybe I'm just bitter.

I was bitter because it felt like everyone in my cohort was getting better internship placements than me. Really, I know that's not true—I knew, realistically, that some other students must have felt just as screwed over as I did, but the moment we got our placements revealed, I felt nothing but resentment that I wasn't born with more connections.

Many of my classmates were from the Big Bend area—had grown up in this school system—so they knew some teacher who was willing to take them on personally as student teachers. Some of them had already worked in the schools as paraprofessionals or education assistants. I hadn't had that chance, because I'd been cranking out my prerequisite classes in two years instead of three. Now, being the youngest future teacher in my program, I still felt like I was behind everyone else.

I'd had part-time jobs, working retail in college and volunteering at summer camps, but those were just to earn money for school. Teaching was going to be my *career*. Which is why I entered into this program to begin with. The university had accepted me on a general merit scholarship, and my chosen major was part of its own school within the university: the college of education. Basically, you'd spend the first few years of college taking your general classes, and in your final year we joined as one big cohort, taking classes that were specific to education—the psychology of learning, teaching methods, and, of course, student-teaching practicum.

It was early fall when we all learned the names of the schools and teachers we'd be working in and with over the course of the year. Big Bend was a big town—some would call it a city.

I certainly would, given that it was five times the size of my hometown. With the demographics of it being a college town and a community for wealthy retired people, the average income of the town/city was pretty high as far as I was concerned. The schools were well-funded, and the students were children of university professors, lawyers, and doctors from the teaching hospital near the university.

Everyone around my table in class was so excited to open their envelopes and pull out the small strips of paper that revealed no more than the name of a school, a teacher, and the contact information. The rest was on us to make the connection. I knew my luck was hard, though, when I opened my envelope and immediately had to ask aloud, "Where's Rocky Middle School?"

A few of my classmates looked up at me, none of their faces certain. They exchanged glances but largely ignored me to continue comparing papers.

"I think that's in Whiteacre," said Adam, who was from Big Bend and going to be student teaching under his former high school English teacher at one of the fanciest schools in the state.

"Whiteacre?" I had to ask. I had lived in Big Bend for more than two years now, but I wasn't terribly familiar with the school district system. As far as I knew, there was Big Bend proper, and the east suburbs, which had their own school district. I had never heard of Whiteacre.

"Yeah, it's on the west side, near the reservoir?" He nodded encouragingly as he said it, but he said it like it was a question. Like that's where he *thought* it was. But his face gave away that this wasn't a good thing. If it was, he would have said it with an exclamation point rather than a question mark.

I'd always had an overactive imagination. At least that's how it felt to me. My grandma described me to her friends as having "a very deep internal life," whatever that meant. I thought it was her excuse for why I was so quiet in their presence. It was better than being called shy. So when Adam said that he thought Rocky Middle School was out in Whiteacre, I imagined a rocky outcrop in the middle of nowhere, a prisonlike school, like a cement block next to a reservoir. My brain was always visual like that—names had images. And Rocky didn't sound pleasant.

I vaguely knew the direction he was talking about, but the reservoir was a good half-hour drive from where I lived and where the campus was.

"Oh, okay." I tried to sound upbeat and not defeated. I tried to rejoin the conversation in a more positive way. "My cooperating teacher sounds good; she's a woman! Her name is Isabella Means."

Despite her name immediately giving me a visceral reaction, I had to be optimistic; a female cooperating teacher was more than I could hope for. Even in this day and age, secondary teaching programs are overrun with men, at least way more than the elementary side of the program, and the social studies part of the cohort was practically a boys club. At my table, there was only one other girl, and the rest were men, most of whom were getting into teaching just to become high school sports coaches. Yeah, a woman for a cooperating teacher was definitely a plus.

The first time I met Mrs. Means, I felt that she lived up to her name. She was a late-middle-aged woman with dark brown hair peppered with a large amount of gray hairs throughout it. The dark and light tones juxtaposed together reminded me of Cruella de Vil, and I tried not to think of her that way, but sometimes the way she wore it up on top of her head looked like she was ready to go hunt for dalmatian puppies.

I really wanted to like Mrs. Means, and in a lot of ways, I did. She didn't take any crap from kids—she'd been at this a long time. She seemed to have a good work-life balance—she didn't let teaching consume her. She traveled a lot and had successfully raised a family. She had a daughter about my age, which she never failed to remind me of. I don't know at what age people start to think it's rude to ask you your age, but clearly twenty-one wasn't old enough for that. People asked me All. The. Time.

I've always looked kind of young. Not in a baby face, youthful look kind of way, but more just that I've always been small. Not freakishly so, but I'm only about five feet tall. I tried to find shoes with a little bit of height to make up for this fact, but regardless, especially working with kids, I was told that I was short just about every day. Middle schoolers weren't shy about what they thought of your appearance.

I don't even have the kind of physique that denotes that you are a grown woman—I don't have voluptuous curves or a strong physical demeanor. I'm small, and it doesn't help me have a strong presence in a room, which is something required of a teacher. I tried really hard to look my age at least. I never tried to dress in a trendy way or look like I was trying to fit in with students. I used to wear a pair of nonprescription glasses with glass lenses just to look more academic, more lived, but I retired them after one of the seventh graders questioned me about them.

Anyway, working with Isabella Means made me feel even younger because she was constantly talking down to me. She couldn't even remember my name.

"Rachel Harding—like the twenty-ninth president of the United States," I said enthusiastically, only partially to flaunt my historical knowledge.

I sometimes threw out lifelines of conversation like that—I pictured flinging a life preserver off the deck of a boat—swinging my whole body with the throw to give it momentum, hoping that the person I threw it to would use it to come closer to me. It rarely worked, so I don't know why I kept trying.

"We'll just call you Miss H," she said without so much as looking up at me. She was filling out a piece of paperwork I had given her on behalf of the university, certifying that she would take me on, although she had obviously already agreed to do so. I wondered idly how much the university paid supervising teachers, because it clearly had to be a high enough amount that would make this cranky lady think I was worth it.

She handed the form back to me and paused in silence, thinking for a moment before speaking. By the way she was looking at me, I knew that what she was going to say wasn't going to be good. She looked like she was sizing me up, looking for a threat. She didn't see any threat in me. "Look, I'm going to be honest," she began. Great start. "I don't know if you can take this. This is a low-income area.

These students are *rough*, some of them are homeless, and some of them come from very broken homes."

I didn't say anything. She didn't seem like she was done with her speech. If I were more outspoken, I would have asked her what she deemed a "broken home" and see what she thinks is so bad about that. It always struck me as odd that people will speak ill of a certain demographic of people without checking their audience first. Just because I was a student at the university didn't mean I wasn't from a low-income area or didn't come from a broken home. At least one of those things was true. It didn't mean I wasn't a good student.

"This is not the Big Bend School District. We don't have the funding those schools have," she continued. "We don't have the boosters. I would know—all my kids went to North Big Bend, and I live in that neighborhood. It isn't the same here. And as quiet and demure as you are, I think the students are going to eat you alive."

Eat me alive. Those words echoed in my head for months. Even as she signed off to take me on, even as I came ready and enthusiastic every day to her classroom, even when I worked to make connections with the students. *Eat me alive, eat me alive.* What did that even mean? It was odd, the position I was in. As a teacher, I should have some degree of power. As a student teacher, I still answered to Mrs. Means as a student myself. I wanted them to respect me, but even if they didn't listen, even if they all failed, what damage could they do to me? That may have been the wrong way to think about it, but how could I go into this worrying about twelve-year-olds wrecking the career path I'd set out for my entire life? I wasn't going to let them take it away from me, and I certainly wasn't going to let Mrs. Means dictate my future. This meant everything to me, and I wasn't going to let anyone take it away from me.

CHAPTER TWO

THE WAY STUDENT teaching works is a gradual release of responsibility. You start by observing, move on to part-time teaching, and eventually take over all of the teacher's workload. At least, that's how it's *supposed* to work. Mrs. Means didn't have quite the same plan for me that the university did.

As the first weeks went on, I was more and more eager to get my practicum over with so I could get my teaching license and work somewhere I felt was better suited to me. I didn't yet know where that might be, but it couldn't be worse than Rocky Middle.

My interest really was in teaching high school—I never really wanted to teach at a middle school. Many of my cohort mates had been placed in high schools, which only made me envy them more. Teaching high school history was my dream. The way I saw it, this year at middle school was just the dues I had to pay—a trial I had to get through.

Mrs. Means wasn't lying when she said this school had a lack of funding. The ceiling tiles, circa the 1950s, were falling down in places, the concrete floors had major holes in them where you would catch your toe and stumble, and the projector images could barely be seen on the wall. The classroom we were in was small, but at least it had windows. The windows, just above the students' (and my) eye level, overlooked the front of the school building, including the walk up to the door. This always bothered me a bit because it meant Mrs. Means could see me coming every morning, yet she made me knock on the front door until the office staff or janitor let me in. Humiliating.

Mrs. Means's desk was the old-school type of teacher desk, huge and made of wood, and it looked like it came off the Mayflower. She had no computer on it because, unlike every teacher I knew, she still took attendance on paper. She had a small laptop hooked up to the projector screen, but she only used it a couple of times a week to project images from the textbook. She was a very by-the-book lady.

Despite the nice windows letting in natural light, the classroom felt like a cave, probably because it was packed. It couldn't have been bigger than an average living room, and yet there were thirty-five desks smushed in as close together as they could be. The physical size of the school definitely was not set up for the number of students that attended it.

As for the students, Mrs. Means insisted that I refer to them that way as opposed to calling them "kids." She said it made them feel more dignified, and if you treated them with respect, then they would give it back. Fat chance.

I never had doubted my interest in pursuing a career in teaching—until I met the students at Rocky Middle School.

Mrs. Means wasn't kidding—they were pretty rough. I knew that many of them had hard home lives, many had a hard time getting to school, and many didn't have enough to eat. The school had even received a grant to provide free snacks every day during second period, and they'd come around with small paper serving boats with some kind of fruit, vegetable, or cracker.

They were always entirely eaten up, kids taking all the leftovers.

Except bell pepper day. Twelve-year-olds weren't big on eating raw bell peppers at 9 a.m. Hey, more for me. Most of the time, I refrained from taking any of their snacks so that some students could get a second helping, but bell pepper day was fair game.

Many of the seventh graders Mrs. Means had in her classes were about my size. Some bigger, some smaller. This was seventh-grade world history, mostly covering ancient Mesopotamia, Egypt, Greece, and Rome. Ideally, we'd end the year as far as the Middle Ages and the Renaissance, but Mrs. Means took so long studying ancient Egypt that I knew we were behind schedule.

Her classes were packed. I watched them file in every day, class after class, as she taught the same thing six times throughout the day. I wondered if that got boring, teaching the same subject all day, every day, for nearly thirty years, but I supposed she must have preferred it that way—it kept the prep work to a minimum.

Thirty-five twelve-year-olds packed in a small classroom with chairs that they can tip back is a madhouse.

Especially when you had kids like bucktoothed Charles, who peed his pants at least twice a week. Somehow, it became my student-teaching duty to escort him down to the office each time, waiting for him to change in the staff bathroom after the secretary provided him with his standby extra pants.

It bothered me that no one seemed concerned with getting to the bottom of the pants wetting—was it because he got nervous? Was he looking for attention? Or was he simply not potty-trained?

No, they didn't care as long as I brought him back to class dry and clean.

Grunt work, I guess. I had to keep telling myself that I was just paying my dues, and when I graduated, it would all be worth it. I just had to get that stellar letter of recommendation from Mrs. Means—she'd be the only one that could vouch for me when it was all said and done. Maybe even the principal here, if I kissed enough ass.

I was never really schmoozy enough, though, to be a networking kind of girl. Schmoozy was my word for anyone who talked just to hear their own voice, just to have the superficial conversations to make people like them. People who bordered on flirty—they were schmoozy. Guys who wanted your number at the bar—they were schmoozy. The people in my teaching program who talked up the professors after every class—they were *so* schmoozy.

I never would have made it in a business position where I'd have to work my way up through socializing. Networking was not my thing. Mrs. Means wasn't wrong in that I was quiet, but that was mostly because I didn't care to have boring conversations, not because I was scared. I'd never really considered myself scared of anything.

CHAPTER THREE

THAT WAS MY life these days—student teaching during the day, my university classes at night. That was the deal for this accelerated teaching program. They set it up for you to get it all done in a year, if you could withstand the pressure. A degree plus all the hours needed for student teaching within a matter of three terms.

My daily schedule was something like this: wake up at six, make myself look presentable and professional, drive the twenty-five minutes it took to the Whiteacre school district, eat a granola bar or banana while merging into and off two different freeway systems, student teach at the behest of Mrs. Means until midafternoon, sometimes later—at the random times she decided she needed me past fifth period—and then done for the day.

Then I scurried back across town, tried to choke down my one real meal of the day, then walked the half a mile from my alleyway apartment to the campus. This apartment was a little sketchy in location, situated right behind a fraternity famous for their legendary parties— I wasn't a fan of the noise, but my roommate,

Lucie, enjoyed the festivities. Cheap, warm beer and yard games didn't seem exceptionally legendary to me, but apparently it did to the near hundreds of people who frequented there every weekend.

No, I didn't choose this house for its ambience or style. I chose this house (and convinced Lucie to go along with it) because it was functionally exactly as I needed it to be for this school year. Two bedrooms, one bath, on-site laundry, two parking spaces, and close enough to the east side of campus to walk to my night classes with reasonable safety.

My classes were held in the education complex—I wasn't sure why they called it a complex when it was only one building—and spanned the evening hours to accommodate our student-teaching schedules. Some days we had two back-to-back classes from 4 to 6, then 6 to 8, but by winter term, when our responsibilities as young teachers ramped up, our classes usually were 7 to 9 p.m.

All of our classes were with the same cohort of classmates from the beginning of the program. Many of us had been going to Big Bend University for the last three years, but some had transferred in for this fourth-year program. Finishing my prerequisite classes in two years had put me ahead.

I don't have a good answer for why I did it—I told people it was a financial choice, trying to enter the workforce quicker to start making money. Really, I didn't do it intentionally. I just liked taking classes, and let's face it, I wasn't the most social college student. With so few distractions, it really wasn't a challenge to complete all my prerequisites to the program in only two years.

So our cohort had become a settled community of key players in set roles. We knew who was outspoken, we knew who were friends, we knew who had the connections in the community, and we knew who was new to the area. I knew a lot about my classmates, but I wasn't sure how well they really knew me.

People have always told me that I'm reserved, and that I come across as quiet or shy. I'm not really shy. I'm not afraid to speak in front of others—otherwise, how could I become a teacher? I'd rather just keep to myself unless I have something vital to say. And I am kind of reserved—I reserved my true self for those closest to me.

That was how I ended up living with Lucie. We'd been paired as random roommates our freshman year (the quintessential college experience, she'd said), and I stuck to her like glue. I'd always been fairly independent and could usually figure things out on my own, but I'd never known anyone who went to college, and her whole family had gone here. She had it dialed in, and it was much easier to follow her lead or ask her for help than flailing and failing miserably.

I convinced her to stick with me, and a year after that, we'd moved into an off-campus apartment together. I'd never been good at making friends, and other than Lucie, I didn't make a single friend in my first year. Or even my second. Maybe if I hadn't had Lucie to fall back on, I would've been forced to branch out, but I was damn glad I hadn't had to figure it all out on my own. Lucie was my college guardian angel and spirit guide.

Sure, she had values that were a little different from mine—she was more into parties and rowdy social events, and she spent most of her time out and around—but she didn't pressure me to change, and she helped me figure out the important things, like financial aid and how to use the printers in the library.

I had coasted through the first two years in Big Bend, with Lucie as basically my only close friend, but I'd met a lot of people through her.

Her girlfriend, Amy, was pretty cool, and she had a lot of interesting characters around her at all times. I didn't hang out with them much, because I got the distinct feeling they thought I was a stick-in-the-mud, and that was okay with me. I hung out with them when I wanted to, and I kept to myself when I needed to. They didn't push me, because they didn't seem to miss me when I was absent.

I had usually been too busy with schoolwork, working at my retail job at the Gap, or daydreaming about my future, when everything would be all sunshine and rainbows and I'd definitely make awesome friends who loved me. I would create the perfect career for myself and surround myself with a community that would love me, and I'd meet a handsome man who would share my values and outlook on life. Maybe he'd be a teacher too, and we'd have summer adventures together.

For now, here I was, a third-year student in a fourth-year college program, sitting here surrounded by guys. Guys who had no interest in dating me. In this program, I mostly hung out with the guys.

I've never been one of those girls—you know, the ones who insist that guys are less drama and that girls hate them for no reason, and so on? I wasn't a tomboy ever. I would have loved a close girl friend; it's just that there weren't as many in my cohort. If I'd joined the elementary track of teacher education, then, boy howdy, would I be surrounded by young women. But I'd never wanted to do that—I never knew how to communicate with young children as well as teenagers. Something about teen angst spoke to me.

In the secondary education cohort, there were plenty of women, but most of them were more specifically on track to become English or science teachers. For social studies, there were only two: me and a girl named Ivy.

If I was being honest, I kind of envied Ivy. I *really* envied Ivy. She was the president of her sorority, so she was very popular on campus and incredibly social, but she also dressed cool and seemed sure of herself. She also had a kickass name. "Ivy" was much cooler than "Rachel."

I didn't try too hard to be friends with Ivy. We had worked together on projects here and there with groups, but Ivy had her own agenda, and it always involved her getting ahead. She was out to network, and I had to give her props for it.

I mostly sat with two guys—Luke and Adam. They had become fast friends early on in the program, as men often do. A superficial friendship where they hardly knew anything about each other but would still blindly follow each other into battle. That's how male friendships looked to me. It was interesting, though, because the two really couldn't be more different: Luke had thick dark curls, while Adam's blond was thinning so severely that I could see his scalp. Luke was tall and thin, and Adam was only a couple inches taller than me. Adam was in a serious relationship with a sweet girl named Haley, and Luke appeared to be perpetually single. Adam was devoutly religious, making time for church every Sunday, while Luke spent his Sundays recovering from his Saturday nights. I was somewhere in between the two of them.

I'd kind of been on the periphery of their bromance from the beginning. We all worked well together, which came in handy for the many group projects we were assigned. Still, I definitely wasn't one of the boys, and I spent most of the time holding my tongue to keep them from being appalled at all the thoughts I had but didn't verbalize. My imagination sometimes got the best of me, but I tried to keep it in check.

Maybe I was judgmental, but I wasn't confrontational. I didn't actually have much to judge Adam for, because he was a pretty decent person. A little smug and privileged, but so were a lot of people in this allegedly prestigious program.

I say the program was only *allegedly* prestigious because of people like Luke.

I judged Luke, only a little. I figured out early on that he was one of the multiple people in our program who had mugshots floating around out in the ether. Not that I was from a family exempt from criminal records, but it was beyond me how so many future teachers had gotten DUIs or been arrested for minor drug crimes or, in Luke's case, disorderly conduct. Were our standards as a society so low? These were the people taking care of our nation's future.

I had to pretend none of it bugged me, though, even when the images swirled in my head of Luke drunkenly disturbing the peace, making a scene, or doing whatever he did that was bad enough to warrant a night in jail. He didn't give exact details of his behavior, but I had no trouble imagining him causing all kinds of ruckus. I could see it. I could see *him*. A danger to society. It was a wonder he wasn't able to talk the officers out of arresting him—he had everyone so wrapped around his freckled fingers that when he told the story of his arrest to a group of us after class one night, no one even seemed appalled. Or maybe they were pretending, like me.

Luke was unabashed, however. He described himself constantly as a "wild card," like no one would ever know what his next move would be. I found it arrogant; most people seemed to find it charming.

So that was our core group: Adam, the smug goody-goody with connections; Miss Out-For-Herself Ivy; Luke, the "wild card" drunk delinquent; Quiet-But-Thinks-A-Lot me; and about two dozen more future teachers who probably also had criminal records or emotional baggage. As a group, though, the camaraderie was something I'd never before experienced. I felt like this group of people understood what I valued—because they valued it too: bettering the face of education, to give kids a home in schools.

That's all I ever wanted.

And then things changed.

CHAPTER FOUR

FRIDAY—THE BEST DAY of the week. It's kind of an unspoken rule that teachers dress more casually on Fridays. Even jeans were common on Fridays, though I couldn't help but notice that Mrs. Means frequently wore jeans during the week anyway. I guess you could get away with a lot more when you'd been teaching as long as she had.

I wondered what it was like for her, being the oldest person on staff. I'd gotten used to being the youngest adult in most rooms, and I couldn't help but wonder how my esteem would be affected when one day that wasn't true. When I wasn't the youngest woman in a position of authority, would I feel threatened? Was Mrs. Means threatened by anyone, or did she simply not care? She was working for people younger than herself—the principal, Mrs. Cairns, couldn't have been older than forty-five. The vice principal was even younger—Ryan was a young father.

I wore my favorite jeans to celebrate the brisk Friday morning, paired with a smart cardigan sweater that was very professional. It came from the haul of clothes I bought while I still had my employee discount at the Gap. I made a huge shopping trip just before I quit to start my teaching program. The jeans were tight enough to make me feel attractive, but not so tight that I looked like I was flaunting anything. The sweater was the perfect shade of powder-blue to match my eyes. A stellar outfit for casual Friday, as long as Charles didn't lose control of his bladder anywhere near me.

I had another reason for wearing my new favorite sweater today—it was the first day that Mrs. Means was letting me teach a whole lesson. We'd gone back and forth for a while about when she would relinquish some of the control to me, but ultimately, we settled for the week after my university sent a formal letter explaining the benchmarks I needed to hit. It was now the beginning of winter term. I should have been teaching full lessons before Thanksgiving break. Mrs. Means still didn't think I was up to it, and it was the first week of January.

Even now, I was to observe her methods for the first two class periods, then try for myself during third period. I couldn't wait. Mostly because I wanted the opportunity to show the students what I knew and could offer them, but also because I needed to show Mrs. Means what I could do. If I could make her respect me, maybe she'd be a little more accepting of me taking over her classroom. I had to do my best today.

The energy of a classroom is always different on a Friday. Students are excited and ready for the weekend. It's better in high schools, where Fridays are usually reserved for pep assemblies and school spirit days, but some of the vibe trickled into middle schools.

My goal that morning, as with any morning, was to be friendly without seeming soft. It was hard to have an air of adulthood about me when I had to wade through a sea of middle school students just to get in the front door. Without a key—even to a side door, where most teachers entered the building—I had to park right out front in the visitor parking spaces and wait outside for the doors to be unlocked, just like anyone else. I was a stranger here. Not a colleague, not a member of the school community. Just a stranger waiting outside for her chance to guest star in the classroom.

As soon as the custodian unlocked the door from the inside, I hustled down the hall in front of the wave of twelve-year-olds. I hightailed it straight to Mrs. Means's classroom and to my desk in the corner. Like with my poor Subaru in the visitor parking, my tote bag, with all my valuables, had no good place to park. I didn't get a drawer or cupboard to close my things in; they sat on the floor under the wooden desk in the corner of the room. The desk itself had no room for belongings, or even to grade papers on. It was piled high with various packets, dusty mementos from past students, and dried-out pens. It was clear that Mrs. Means didn't spend any more time in this classroom than necessary. Once the final bell rang, she was out of there. Again, it made me wonder why she would take on a student teacher. If she wasn't going to spend any more time than necessary at her job, then why take on another responsibility?

Today's lesson was going to be on the split of the Roman Empire. Mrs. Means knew her stuff, I'd give her that. She had been teaching the same content for so long that she knew it front to back. Seventh-grade ancient world history covered the classics: Egypt, Greece, Rome, and the medieval period. She gave students packets to complete while she talked through the material. She wasn't high-tech in the way that my school preached was best. She didn't make PowerPoint presentations or create hands-on activity lessons. She was incredibly consistent in her ability to make every lesson as boring as possible for twelve-year-olds. I mean, really, I had to suffer through her ruining ancient Egypt for me. I couldn't help but think that she was doing a great job of showing me what *not* to do.

After watching Mrs. Means teach her incredibly dull lesson to first and second period, I was feeling confident about executing it third period. The nerves kicked in a bit toward the end of second period—not because I was worried I would misspeak or make a fool of myself, but because I knew Mrs. Means was doubtful, and I knew she had never heard me talk louder than my "demure" speaking voice. I had something to prove, and the time had come.

The bell rang for second period to end, and I went to wait outside the door to welcome students to class. Mrs. Means never joined me in this, but in my program, I had written multiple papers about how this was the best practice for making students feel welcomed in the space. I had just exited the classroom, into the hallway, when I heard it.

A gunshot rang out down the hall from the front of the school.

I stopped hearing anything after that. I stopped breathing, completely frozen.

My ears barely registered that a second shot fired almost immediately after the first, but my head was clouded with a numb sound, like white noise.

The students walking toward me went rigid. Automatically, my body moving without my brain registering my movements, I ushered those who were just outside the door quickly into the room before I glanced back down the hall. The halls were clearing. I turned around and slammed the classroom door, making students inside jump in their seats.

"What are you doing?" Mrs. Means asked me just as the intercom clicked on.

"Teachers—lockdown. I repeat, we are on immediate lockdown."

"What is going on?" Mrs. Means demanded of me, like this was my fault. She hadn't heard it—how had she not heard it?

My mouth opened to speak without my permission, my body still on autopilot. My mouth rushed through my sentence with the anxiety of the situation. "There were gunshots."

Her mouth formed an "O," but no sound came out as she glanced around the room. Not all students had made it to class yet, just a few early birds. They were silent. I looked at them, but I had to quickly look away. I couldn't look at their terror. I had to pretend to be brave.

"We should find something to cover the windows," I said in a low, monotone voice to Mrs. Means, as calmly as possible. "Do you have anything?"

She glanced around. Another side effect of her tenure—she wasn't prepared for twenty-first-century problems. I'd gone to school post-Columbine—I'd done lockdown drills my entire life. I had even been locked down for real a few times—but never had I heard actual shots fired anywhere near me.

Time seemed to be moving very slowly. We told our few students, in hushed tones, to move into the corner and sit quietly. As they squatted and hunkered down, Mrs. Means and I quickly taped pieces of construction paper together until it covered the window on the door. I couldn't hear anything else in the hallway, and I didn't see anyone through the glass as we covered it. What was going on out there? Had it been minutes or mere seconds?

Was there an active shooter in our midst? Were they right outside the door in the hallway?

Most importantly, had anyone been hurt? Would any of my students get hurt?

The thought made me sick to my stomach. I felt like puking. Seeing my cowering students from the corner of my eye, I straightened my back and held my composure, moving to the corner where they were on the ground behind desks. I sat at a desk in front of them. Mrs. Means sat at her own desk at the front of the room. She didn't seem scared or concerned—maybe this wasn't her first experience with this sort of thing.

We sat there silently for what felt like hours. It could have been just a few minutes. The adrenaline pumping through all of our veins wasn't helping to keep us calm, but the students were silent. They didn't touch one another. They didn't hug. They didn't smack or pinch each other, the way I saw them interacting all day, every day. They sat silently, occasionally looking up at me with the saddest, most terrified eyes. I knew immediately I would never forget those eyes.

Maddie, a small girl with frizzy brown hair, got my attention and whispered, "Miss H, can I get my phone? I want to text my mom."

I looked to Mrs. Means. She hadn't heard. As quietly as I dared, I stood up and crossed the classroom to where she was seated, repeating Maddie's question in her ear. She nodded.

Moving across the room on my tiptoes and hunched over, feeling like I might have to throw myself to the ground any second, I moved back across the room. Instead of returning to Maddie immediately, I veered toward where my own bag was and grabbed my phone.

I tiptoed back to the student corner and whispered back at Maddie. She nodded and whispered back, cupping her hands around her mouth like a small child.

I crossed to her binder, sitting atop her desk. Maddie was a good student, always organized, always polite. That was why she'd been to class early—and it might have saved her life today. I unzipped her binder slowly, trying to cut out any noise despite the fact that we hadn't heard so much as footsteps coming down our hall.

Her phone was right inside her front pocket. Strictly speaking, the middle schoolers weren't allowed to have their phones in class. But we all knew they snuck them in somehow. I was grateful for it today, if only to give them something to pacify and comfort them.

Then came the sirens.

There were so many police sirens.

I'll never forget the sound of the sirens.

How could people live in cities where sirens were so commonplace? They set me on edge on a good day, let alone when I was in a school. A place that was meant to be safe for these students, not a place that sirens lead to.

"It's probably a domestic dispute," Mrs. Means said quietly after a few minutes, "a disagreement that got out of hand. That happens sometimes in this neighborhood. It most likely has nothing to do with the school."

I hoped she was right, but I had my doubts. The shots sounded like they were right outside. The windows were above my eye level, but I could hear commotion outside. If there weren't students watching my every move, I might have moved a chair to peek outside.

We sat for an eternity longer. With my phone in hand, I quietly flipped through all breaking news outlets in Big Bend, searching for any announcement about what had happened. I texted my grandma—not about the lockdown or to say I was okay but because I wanted to have someone to text.

I also texted Lucie, wondering if she could find out what was happening. She hadn't heard anything.

The students were actually holding up well. Maybe not surprising, considering the amount of trauma so many of these students had already faced in their lives. But still, I was amazed at how well-contained many of them seemed. They were still huddled into desks on one side of the room, not being silent but staying relatively quiet and calm.

They were entirely too used to this kind of threat—this kind of violence right under their noses.

Mrs. Means was sitting on her laptop, and she appeared to be working on some lesson plans or something. She seemed so unbothered! That was until the next sound paused us all. It started as a low rumble but quickly got louder and louder as the culprit clearly got closer to our location. A beating noise that was above the school, but low.

A helicopter.

A helicopter flying over the school? I was about to ask Mrs. Means what she made of it when my phone vibrated in my hand. A message from Lucie: *News live broadcast of the school—saying they're not sure yet what happened but that it's locked down for student safety.*

I didn't bother to message back before I looked up to Mrs. Means. "It looks like they're news helicopters—they're live reporting on this."

"Shit" was Mrs. Means's only reply. Her eyes had a vacant look. A few students gasped and looked up, probably never having heard her curse before, but they were quickly reabsorbed in their phone screens.

One girl, Kaylie, began to get upset. Panicky. She was in the tightest corner, a little blond girl in a bright yellow T-shirt. She started crying.

I looked to Mrs. Means, who didn't get up from her chair but had noticed Kaylie's distress.

When it became clear that Mrs. Means wasn't going to do anything, I moved. I got up and silently moved to Kaylie's side, squatting next to her.

I've never been a touchy person, but I tentatively reached out a hand and rubbed her shoulder.

"It's going to be okay, Kaylie," I said quietly. I sat with her, among the pile of students.

More information was released shortly thereafter. Police were surrounding the school due to an armed shooter situation.

No students were harmed.

That was all that mattered to me. That, and when could we get out of this room?

It was announced over the intercom that we could relax a bit; we were on "lockout" mode instead of "lockdown," meaning that we could make a bit more noise and move about the classroom, but still no one was permitted to open their doors.

Students began to complain of needing to use the restroom, but really, I think we were all just getting a bit stir-crazy.

Mrs. Means took it upon herself to venture out first. I was left with the room of fifteen students, all of whom were on edge and close to panicking, while she went to use the restroom and scope out the situation. I kept close by the door, waiting to open it back up for her when she got back. Hoping she had more information.

She did.

When she returned, she didn't follow me into the room. She gestured for me to follow her out to the hall. I was usually a strict rule follower, but she was kind of my boss.

"It's the parent of a student," she began without any preface, but we both knew what she meant.

"He came to argue about some custody thing. He pulled a weapon, and the resource officer shot him. The body is out front."

I was stunned beyond language. My mouth was hanging open like an idiot. We were both silent for a beat as I processed what she'd said. My heart seemed to flutter in my chest, and I felt like I might break down like Kaylie.

"Do we know the student?" I asked, my mind suddenly taking a mental inventory of which students were in the stronghold of the classroom.

"No, he's an eighth grader. You wouldn't know him, but I had him last year. He's already been pulled from class and is with the mother."

It at least gave me some relief that the child who had lost a parent today wasn't in my midst, but a cloud still hung over me as the words sunk in.

Someone had been shot and killed at our school building today.

CHAPTER FIVE

Hours passed. Students couldn't leave. The school phone lines were ringing nonstop with parents trying to collect their child from the school that was on the news. I wished someone wanted to come get me.

It was midafternoon, and no one had gotten any lunch. We were still being held in our classrooms.

If my anxiety wasn't high enough already, it was getting worse because I had class later. It was already 2 p.m. I would usually be headed home by now.

I wasn't needed at the school anymore. Things had calmed down enough that nearly every room was playing some form of TV show on the projector to keep students entertained—or keep them from panicking.

It had become my job to escort students back and forth from the bathroom, steering them clear of the front of the school, where they were putting some sort of plastic covering over the front windows so students couldn't see the tarp-covered body out front, along with the stream of blood pooling out from under it.

I'd spent the last hour and a half covering the class of an English teacher named Mr. Tyler, who left *Looney Toons* playing. After this day, I didn't think I'd ever watch Wile E. Coyote again. He'd had to step out to collect himself and left the twenty-one-year-old student teacher in charge.

If others were allowed to step out, then I felt I should be able to bow out early after covering for them all day. I needed to leave. As soon as they found someone else to cover for Mr. Tyler (the librarian, it turned out), I asked Mrs. Means to advocate on my behalf to the principal, or the state police, or whoever had the authority to let me drive my car out of the lot.

No was the answer I got back. I couldn't go. The parking lot was an active police scene, and as my car was front and center in visitor parking, it was directly behind the police crime scene tape.

After some back-and-forth, the caveat reached was that I could go if I could find someone to come and get me and if I snuck out the back doors and across the back sports field, whereas not to draw attention to the fact that someone was leaving. Not when students weren't yet allowed to leave.

I understood that parents were upset and wanted to see and hug their children. After a tragic event, students have to be systematically released to their families in something called "the reunification process." It's supposed to be a very delicate and emotional time, especially after all the worry and stress of whatever causes the reunification to be necessary.

I knew all about it, theoretically, as reunification after a traumatic event was all too commonplace in schools these days. Learning about it had become mandatory in teacher preparation programs. I didn't think too much about why, or whether that would ever be me.

I didn't want to facilitate the reunification process. I was just selfish enough to want to get out early. But that meant finding a ride home. Of course, I only had one person to call.

I texted Lucie to see if she could come get me: *Hey, they're letting me go, but I need a ride home. If I send you the address, do you think there's any chance you could come get me?*

I stared at my phone until I saw the three little dots that meant she was typing.

I'll be like twenty minutes, then I'll leave. Where is it?

I wished she was eager to come get me as soon as possible. I wished she was rushing to come get me the second I was released, like she was concerned about my well-being. I couldn't make her understand how badly I wanted to get out of this building. The image of the tarp covering a body in the threshold was almost too much for me—I could hardly think about anything else.

I had spent my day being a strong face, and I was hitting my limit. I was about to break. After sending Lucie the address, I left. It took almost half an hour to drive to Rocky from our apartment, and I knew she barely would have left by now. Despite knowing she wouldn't be there for at least another twenty minutes, I started walking. I grabbed my pile of belongings and headed out the back door of the building.

As I emerged into the bright day, unseasonably blue-skied for January, I didn't look up at the helicopters flying above. I didn't dare look behind me, seeing the police cars, the ambulance that was unnecessary, the news stations reporting, or the parents anxiously waiting for a glimpse of their child.

I didn't see any of that.

With my arms full of papers to grade over the weekend, I walked briskly down the long stretch of sidewalk, trying to keep the tears from escaping my eyes. I walked, and I walked, and I walked.

I had made it over a mile before Lucie's sedan rounded the corner up ahead and headed straight toward me. I was walking on the side of the street I knew she'd be coming from so I could just hop into the passenger seat when she pulled over.

As her car grew nearer, I started failing my arms wildly, like a stranded desolate on an island who saw a ship in the distance. Sobs began escaping my lips as my freedom got closer. And closer. Just when I could see her face clearly through the windshield, my tears unstoppable now, she didn't glance at me once as she passed by.

She drove down the road past me, and I grew to hysterics, hyperventilating in between sobs. Lightheaded, I had to crouch to the ground, squatting as my knees grew weak. I didn't think once about the cars passing by me, the people waiting by the bus stop across the street. I didn't care what they saw, what they thought of me.

My phone rang. Lucie. I answered but didn't get any words out before she said, "Where are you?"

"Y-y-you p-p-passed me," I stammered out. Standing up, I turned and saw where she had driven down a few blocks and was turning around. I hung up as I ran across the street to her side of the road. I hadn't looked both ways while crossing like Grandma always told me to.

Fortunately, no one had been too close. I made it to where the bus stop was stationed by the time Lucie was pulling up. I must have looked like a wreck, because she got out of her car and jogged over to me to help me carry my papers. I didn't give her the papers. I grabbed her and hugged her while I kept sobbing.

She didn't say anything as she broke the hug and guided me to her car, put me inside, and closed my door before running over to her side and getting in.

I was shaking, shaking hard. Though my tears had somewhat waned, my body shook as though sobs were racking through me. It must have been noticeable because Lucie turned the heat up. We rode in silence for a few minutes until she asked me, "Do you need something to eat? You texted that you didn't get lunch. Want to run through McDonalds?"

I could tell Lucie was uncomfortable. She didn't know what to say to me. I didn't feel like eating in the least. But I quietly nodded and let her drive me through the drive-through. She ordered me fries, chicken nuggets, and a large soda pop. She paid without even asking for my debit card as I rode in the passenger seat, staring ahead as my mind was somewhere else. Or nowhere else. I was numb.

I sipped at my Coke but didn't touch the food. Not even when we got home, when I thanked Lucie for the ride and trudged up the stairs to my room, leaving her standing alone at the bottom. I closed my door, laid on the bed, and cried.

CHAPTER SIX

I WENT TO CLASS. I had to go to class.

It was the first day of a new class, one that only met once a week. I had to go. I couldn't afford to be a week behind.

I peeled myself off my bed and put myself together. I took off the powder-blue sweater and jeans that I'd left feeling so confident in that morning and changed into some leggings and a big sweatshirt. Maybe if I looked comfortable, I'd feel comfortable. I never dressed so casually for class—I didn't feel it helped my image as someone trying not to look like the youngest person in the room.

But that Friday, I didn't care how I looked. I barely bothered to wash off the mascara that had run down my cheeks. I didn't reapply any either. I put my stringy, flat hair up in a sloppy ponytail, grabbed my bag and laptop, and set off to class on foot.

I didn't immediately regret going to class, not even when I walked in and the room fell silent. Of course they all knew. We all knew where each other were student teaching; we had to talk about it consistently to debrief our experiences. That hadn't helped me feel less resentful of their superior placements before, and it certainly wouldn't now.

I ignored the staring faces as I found a seat toward the side of the room. I never liked sitting in the middle of a room; it always felt claustrophobic to me to be directly surrounded by people. Today I found a seat on the far side at an empty table. If I came to class early, I always gambled by sitting at a table alone, setting a trap to see who would sit by me.

The few other early birds resumed their conversations. The professor was nowhere to be seen. Annabel McAdams, her name was. I was curious to see her, especially because all of our methods class teachers so far had been men. Hearing from a woman on how to run a classroom would be an interesting comparison.

Members of my cohort filed in, no one daring to speak to me, but I could feel their eyes. I kept my head low, not wanting to advertise the puffy redness of my eyes, giving them the satisfaction of knowing I was so upset.

Did I have a right to be upset? I was okay; my students were okay. It wasn't a school shooting—but what was it? A shooting-type incident? I didn't know enough yet to form an opinion on the ethics of it, I guess. That bugged me most of all—the not knowing. What to feel, what to say, how to act.

Was I allowed to be hurt, or would it be more couth of me to act like I was okay?

I didn't have time to decide before I was engaged for the first time. Daniel, the tall guy with glasses who was placed in the Whiteacre District as well. Of course, I could still resent him, because at least he was teaching English at the *high school* down the road from Rocky. I was resentful of everyone at the moment.

"Hey, you okay?" he said, leaning over me. "We were locked down today too. Pretty scary, huh?"

I dared to look up at him. Though my chest was tight, I gave him my best possible small smile.

"Yeah, I'm okay. Thanks. I didn't see much. If I had, I'd probably be a lot more upset."

I don't know why the lie came out. Maybe because I knew everyone was eavesdropping, maybe because I wanted everyone to look away, and thinking that I was okay and had nothing to report would be the best way to drop their attention.

Or maybe because I wished it was true, that I could feel like him and simply have had a little scare of a lockdown today. Not that I heard the fatal shots of someone's murder a dozen feet away from me.

That seemed to satisfy him, though, because he gave me a reassuring nod and a small smile after saying, "Good, I'm glad. I'm happy you're okay." He walked away.

I knew Daniel was a nice guy. I knew he had a long-term girlfriend, who he called his "partner," which felt really respectful to me. He was even pretty cute, and he had a nice sense of humor that was subtle but nuanced. I appreciated him a lot, but I was happy to have dismissed him. Especially because Luke had just walked in.

Of course, Luke didn't stare at me like the others did. In fact, he didn't acknowledge me at all. He came in and took his seat across from me at our table, which had since been populated by a couple of the other regulars who hadn't even tried to say hi to me.

I knew I could count on Luke to be nonchalant—it was his whole cool-guy act. I was still skeptical that it was for real.

I was silently begging Luke to say something normal to me, when a tall woman with wild hair walked in. She had to be Annabel McAdams.

She was built big, with a broad body type and lots of curves. Her curly hair, which was so dark brown that it was almost black, contrasted heavily with her stunningly bright blue eyes that bugged out of her head. I suspected she dyed her hair that dark to achieve the effect, and it worked wonderfully.

She wore such muted dark clothes that her eyes were the brightest color on her person. She towered over the class before her.

She had just set her bag down on the podium when she looked up at the class and said, "Okay, which one of you is Rachel?"

I stopped breathing. Everyone's eyes locked onto my back. I didn't bow my head down but rather turned my gaze directly at Annabel McAdams. I lifted my hand slightly into the air and said, "I am."

She let out a big exhale, almost like a chuckle, with a slight smile on her face. "Phew, sounds like you've had a rough day, huh?"

I couldn't believe it. Here I was, trying to pretend it had been a usual day for me, and my teacher decided to introduce herself to me in the most mortifying way possible. My cheeks burned. No, they more than burned. They'd already felt hot from crying all afternoon. My entire body simmered with the humiliation of being called out on what had been the worst day of my life.

My hoodie suddenly felt too tight, and my stomach tightened. I thought I might puke, but luckily I hadn't ingested much that day. I couldn't get a word out in response. Much to my dismay, I muttered something between an "mmhmm" and a "yeah."

I felt like a child. A small, helpless child who couldn't speak for herself. I didn't have to say anything else, though, because Annabel was continuing on. "I sure know what that's like. My first ever week of teaching fourth-grade, September eleventh happened. That was rough."

Again, I didn't have a reply. It's kind of like the Holocaust—when someone brings up the Holocaust as a comparison, what else is there really to say? In America, nothing trumped the terrorist attack on 9/11. Nothing had ever left everyone so shaken, so scared. But I had barely even been alive then, so again I kept my mouth shut. Who had sold me out to her? Had one of my cohort mates mentioned it to her without me noticing? Or did the program administrators warn her to look out for me? If that was the case, I guessed it was only a matter of time before they reached out to me.

I was contemplating what I might say to Josephine if she

requested a conference with me. Josephine was the head coordinator for the program—the real head honcho. She oversaw everyone's student-teaching placement, kept an eye on our class involvement and grades, and had the ultimate say in if we met the qualifications for our teaching licenses in June. Some students built personal relationships with Josephine, but I'd always remained quiet around her. She seemed like the type of woman whose time you didn't want to waste, but she was approachable enough.

Annabel kept talking. She continued to introduce herself, explaining that she was a mother of two, taught elementary school for ten years, then high school English for another eight. She was now a doctoral student, finishing up her dissertation in race relations in American schools. I could see some of my classmates already starting to adore her, but I'd made my mind up. Annabel could get fucked.

Class lasted for two hours that night—7 to 9 p.m. Who at the University of Big Bend's registrar office scheduled a course from 7 to 9 on a Friday night? I didn't know, but I was sure that I would never be on my best game for that class. I sat through her first hour of lecture, thinking about everything but the lecture.

I think she was talking about integrity in our craft or being an authentic person or something when she announced that we were going to break for half an hour to write a poem about ourselves, the likes of which we would share with the class after the break. Since she encouraged us to lounge about the building for optimum inspiration, I was out of the classroom door without another beat.

I squeaked down the hall in my stiff tennis shoes, another side effect of dressing up most of the time. When you wear sneakers, you feel self-conscious. Especially if they still need to be broken in. The education building was relatively new—only a few years in operation. Thus, it had all the fancy features that tuition money pays for: a mini coffee shop in the lobby, a catwalk for an upstairs hallway, and my target location for the evening, a double-sided gas fireplace. I parked myself on the bench in front of one side.

The heat was glorious—I hadn't realized how chilled I felt. I had brought nothing but my notepad and my pencil. I leaned against the pillar behind me, bending my knees up to write against it. It felt good to be scrunched into a ball; it felt safe. I usually wouldn't be caught in such a childlike position in public—it didn't go with my sophisticated adult image. I stared at my paper. How was I supposed to write a poem about who I was when I didn't really feel like myself?

I don't know how long I was staring at my paper before Adam and Luke walked up, followed closely by another couple of classmates.

"Yes, the fireplace! Exactly where I was headed," Adam said, forever the comrade. I mumbled my reply, not being too friendly, partially because I genuinely didn't feel friendly and partially because I came to the fireplace to be alone. Also, to get warm.

They formed a circle around me—or, rather, around the fireplace—some on the floor, some perched in chairs they brought over. They began discussing their poems and what they were thinking for them. I was just glad they didn't come over to ask me anything or bother me.

Some of them took turns reading aloud what they'd written so far. I kept quiet. Adam looked like he was about to ask me something, but Luke stole everyone's attention by reading his poem aloud:

"'He's a wild card,' they say." He paused for some chuckles. Luke, the performer. He continued.

> And he'll never live up to his name,
> Luke Earnest: the slickest in the game.
> If he can't get anywhere with his sweet talk alone,
> He'll make it because of his brain.
> Never the favorite—the second-born son,
> Doing all he can to become number one.
> Gotta make it as a poet, so I won't teach for long,
> I'll steal your mind with a lesson, and your heart with a song.

Trying to find my way
I'll take any job that pays.
I'll make them all proud.
He's a wild card, they say.

Adam began criticizing him on his rhyming structure immediately, but his self-reflection got me thinking about my own. What does it say about us, the way we present our own self-image?

It was 8:30 on the dot when Annabel called us back together in the classroom to read our poetry. I usually was the type to volunteer to read first, just to get it over with, and if I'm being honest, I liked to show off that I was brave enough. It made a statement to be the first to step up—not to wait and be in the middle, not to be the reluctant last one.

Today, I wasn't the brave one. Maybe my bravery had worn thin. I waited until there was a beat of hesitation among the rest of the group and quietly raised my hand. I didn't stand up. I didn't raise my voice above my speaking voice.

"Where I Come From" by Rachel Harding:
From needing something just out of reach
To grasping for straws anywhere they lay,
Trying to find my place in the crowd
And standing alone at the end of the day.
From hand-me-downs that never quite fit
And groups of people that fit the same,
Being proud of myself when others weren't.
Above average intellect, with a below average name.
From the long stays at Grandma's that turned into my home,
The strife to which I've never shirked.
From going back-to-back to show that I'm small
And the words that do the same when that doesn't work,
I'm from the place that I don't admit

And never settling for less than magnificent,
Wishing, wishing, wishing I could be somewhere else,
Someone else, anything different.

I didn't look around the room when I was done. I kept my gaze low, except for the one glance up just long enough to catch Luke's stare. He wasn't looking at me with pity or concern. He was looking at me with a different expression than I'd ever seen him wear. Was it interest? Intrigue? His eyes were soft, his lips barely parted. He didn't applaud with the others—he just stared.

My cheeks felt hot again, but differently than before. I was no longer embarrassed at the attention of everyone else—I was shy from the attention from Luke alone.

CHAPTER SEVEN

I DIDN'T LISTEN TO music on my way to school that Monday morning. I drove in silence on the surprisingly clear morning. It should have been raining; that would have fit the mood better. It was sunny, despite being no later than 7:15 a.m. I had to get to school early because Mrs. Means had called me Sunday night to tell me we had a staff meeting first thing to debrief on Monday. Great.

She had called me twice that weekend—the only two times she had ever called me.

She called me late Friday night, after I had returned home from class. I didn't answer. I didn't want to deal with anyone else that night. That didn't stop me from listening to her voicemail, though—bumbling her way through concern. "I, uh, just wanted to, um, make sure that you're okay, and, um, if you have any questions about today, um, please give me a call. Thank you. Goodbye."

I didn't call back. I mean, she wasn't the emotional type before. Why should I lean on her now?

She called again Sunday night to tell me to be there early for the meeting. Nothing else was said, and the phone call lasted about fifteen seconds.

When I pulled into the school parking lot, I noticed cop cars. Three of them, to be exact, all parked out front in the visitor parking. My parking. I noticed the way I didn't want to look at the front of the school. It felt wrong, like staring at someone with a deformity or something. Gawking at something I shouldn't linger on. To be a good person, I shouldn't be gawking, but I almost couldn't help it. I didn't want to look at where it had happened, and how the windows to our classroom were mere feet away, but that's all I could think about. It was probably all anyone could think about.

I had worn my new sweater to make me feel good. I always tried to dress for my mood, but I didn't spend a bunch of time investing in my appearance. That was part of the whole "trying to be older than I really am" thing; I couldn't look like I was trying too hard to be pretty or appealing, or no one would take me seriously. Not the students, not Mrs. Means, and certainly none of my colleagues.

So I generally dressed pretty drab—not unflattering, but just put together enough to look pleasing. Today was different, though. I needed to feel good about myself, and I needed to feel secure. I'd dress the part for sure—my new sweater was the key.

After I got home from class on Friday night, I wanted to put on my favorite Disney movie and cry until I fell asleep, but first there was the matter of collecting my car.

I had Lucie drive me across town again, thankful that she hadn't gone out yet that night. If there was ever a night I needed her with me, it was now.

My car was the last one in the lot, save for the police deputy on watch. He shined his flashlight toward me as Lucie dropped me off and I climbed in my car. He seemed satisfied enough and didn't approach me, but I drove away quickly anyway. I couldn't stomach a cop talking to me after that day. Knowing what they carried and what they were capable of.

I had trouble sleeping that night. Despite turning up my heater and wrapping myself in the blanket my grandma made for me, I couldn't stop shivering.

My puffy eyes, on Saturday morning, must have been significant, because they notified Lucie that I needed a day out. She took me to the mall that I very seldom visited—because I was a college student on a budget—but Lucie frequented it often. She liked to buy the overpriced candles at Bath & Body Works, then not burn them. They piled in the corner of her room like trophies.

Following our shopping binge, I had splurged on two new pairs of shoes (one practical and one just because they were cute), as well as a new knit sweater with sewn-on elbow patches. Very teachery, very me. And very fun, because it was a bright shade of mustard-yellow. I was feeling good—until I walked into the staff meeting.

Walking through the halls to the library felt like it was in slow motion. The halls felt strangely empty and quiet.

I tried to greet everyone pleasantly, with a smile and a "good morning," but I was mostly met with wide eyes and mumbled hellos. It was then that I noticed that every member of the staff was wearing a similar T-shirt. Black, with a school logo on the front. Clearly, school T-shirts of past years, whatever they had from their years of tenure.

We were mourning. And I was wearing bright yellow.

I was the brightest in the room, and I quickly felt that my attempt to feel secure had made me stand out in the worst way.

Did I look callous? What could I possibly say? That I had worn the sweater to make myself feel more confident? I wasn't a staff member—I didn't get the group emails planning acts of solidarity. I chose to think that that's what was behind the matching group aesthetic, not that everyone but me had simultaneously had the same thought, and I was the jerk wearing sunshine to a funeral. *I'm sorry, Sammie,* I thought.

It had come out in the press on Saturday that the parent who was killed was named Sammie. The father of the eighth-grade boy, Shane, who I indeed did not know. Sammie used they/them pronouns, which made this a lot more complicated.

In my social-justice-oriented program of study, I had read enough literature to know (not to mention taken enough sociology classes for the guilt to last a lifetime) that an act of police violence against a nonbinary person was sure to be a legal and political mess. Sammie was also not White—it was not yet announced their full background, but we knew some things.

Sammie had been a social-justice activist for violence against people of color. Absolutely none of this was shaping up to be a simple situation. They had organizations full of allies ready to go.

I was eager to hear what the school had to say—how we'd proceed, who was to blame. I noted that the school resource officer wasn't present. He was probably in jail, right? Were we going to mourn the loss of Sammie, express the school's regrets, and make amends? Was that the politically correct thing to do? More importantly, was that the *right* thing to do?

My fall term English Language Arts methods class had collectively read *The Hate U Give*. We (a room of mostly White people) discussed in detail the implications of police violence against people of color. We'd read peer-reviewed studies of the school-to-prison pipeline and held Socratic seminars about the high homicide and suicide rates of trans and nonbinary people. I knew how I should feel about this. I knew how the media would react.

I took my usual seat toward the front of the library. Mrs. Means came hustling through the door at the last minute. When all the black T-shirt wearers were seated, four policemen stood at the front of the room.

Trauma responses are all the same. Not individual peoples' responses—they couldn't be more different. I learned that very quickly. Hell, I learned that in the first five minutes of the most traumatic event of my life. People will surprise you with how they handle situations, whether they withdraw into themselves or act out against some external force—anything to cope with the emotions that bubble up.

No, the trauma response of the institution, of the media, of the people in charge—it's always the same. It felt extremely impersonal to have these police, who I felt a tinge of fear from, stand up in front of this particular group of people and say their piece, like reading it from a script.

It was the principal, Mrs. Cairns, dressed in a black Rocky Middle shirt herself, who began by reading us the message on the paper in her hands, as if the district had handed it right to her and ordered her to read it word for word:

> Together, our school community has witnessed an unthinkable tragedy. As we process our emotions and learn how to move forward, many people may feel upset or unwell, and this is normal. Should you have any feelings that you need to process today, please let the admin know that you need to step out. We will be ready to assist you and your classes in any way you may need as we readjust back into our school day.
>
> After a tragedy, it is important to resume routines. Please follow your usual class schedule as usual, but maintain grace for the students, as some of them might have a hard day. We want to get everyone back to feeling normal and safe as smoothly as possible. Please encourage students to express their feelings and know that our counselor is on standby for any who might need support.

That was it. That was their formal statement.

This horrific thing had happened in our workplace, and this is all we had to go off to recover.

I knew that she meant it when she said administrators would step in to cover us for a few minutes today if we needed it, but at the same time I knew that not only would no single teacher call in that help, but the admin would probably be elsewhere anyway.

Just like they were last Friday. Who was left to take over classes when the teacher needed a moment to collect themselves? Me, the student teacher. I felt the weight bearing down on me already.

Mrs. Cairns looked up at her staff sitting before her, seeming to be done. She added, off script, "Ryan will come around to pass out copies of the prepared statement for you to read to your first period, to establish unity as a staff."

Indeed, the vice principal was working his way through the tables, passing out the formal statements like worksheets.

The police chief, the same one that I saw on the news last Friday, spoke next. She was a stocky woman, in her mid-forties, with her hair tied back severely.

"This is kind of a dicey subject, I'm not going to sugarcoat it for you," she said blatantly. "The perpetrator in question identified as a non-gender-binary person and was also Hispanic. Large news outlets could easily blow this story up and implicate us all a lot worse than we already have been. It's really in the best interest of all of us if you don't speak to any press or spread inside knowledge of this far outside of our school community." She paused and looked around, not really making eye contact with any one of us. "Thank you. Let me know if there are any questions."

I hated the way she spoke to the school staff like we were one with the police department. I didn't feel like I was on their side. Were there sides to choose? I was used to everything seeming so clear—so black-and-white. So obvious to me what was right or wrong.

Frank, an Indigenous Kickapoo man from Oklahoma, raised his hand and gently cleared his throat, as gently as a six-foot-four, three-hundred-pound man could.

He had once offered me teaching advice I'd never forget. He was a twenty-year science teacher, and he had told me the first time I'd met him that the thing to keep in mind with students was to not intimidate them—to keep your physical demeanor warm and accessible and not domineering. I still laughed to myself about it today.

Like, did Frank not at all realize that he and I were not the same in that regard? Coming across as domineering and aggressive was the least of my worries in the classroom.

"Yes—you there." The police chief called on him, gesturing with her whole hand but not pointing.

"Thank you. I just wanted to say," Frank began solemnly and softly, "I will be spreading tobacco and smudging sage out front this afternoon after school. If anyone would like to accompany me or join in with me, you are more than welcome. Thank you."

With that, we were dismissed. As we walked down the hall back to Mrs. Means's classroom, she was talking strategy. She didn't seem emotional or bothered—almost like she'd experienced things like this before. It unsettled me. She was the war general incarnate.

"We'll play it by ear today. After we read the prepared statement to first period, we'll gauge how much content they can handle. It'll have to be a mixture of our standard content, to keep it natural and routine, with the understanding that they might not act like themselves today. We'll see how it goes."

She didn't ask me what I thought. We continued on to class.

They let the students in early, without making them wait outside. Of course they couldn't wait outside—not when there were blood stains on the sidewalk. The administrators and the counselor were corralling them inside the doors.

We didn't have much of a chance to breathe before we were overwhelmed by students pouring in the room, including pee-pants Charles, who wet himself before class even began.

I was rereading our statement that we were going to have to give at the beginning of first period when Mrs. Means approached me.

"Do you want to read it, or shall I?" she asked.

I really, really, really didn't want to read it. She must have read that in my eyes, but still I said, "I'll read it. You know the students well, so you can monitor their reactions and see if they need anything." She nodded. She seemed to approve. She took a big breath.

"Well, let's be honest, this will all look fantastic on your résumé. You'll have more experience with trauma than anyone else on the job market, and if you can handle the students after all of this, the recommendation letter I'll write will get you a job anywhere."

Right, my résumé. The mention of it actually surprised me that I wasn't thinking of it myself, especially considering I was aching to get out of this place. All I was thinking of today was moving forward. Getting by, getting through today, little by little, and seeing the students feel comfortable again. Their faces on Friday had been haunting me since.

If Friday felt like an eternity, then Monday felt like the second longest teaching day I'd ever had. Each class dragged by, and I felt myself watching the clock, waiting for each minute to tick by. Many students were absent, which meant that we'd just have to start the process of healing anew with each day that more students came back.

If they ever came back. Parents were probably putting in transfer forms across town in the better school districts if they could. I would be.

As I walked out that afternoon, I passed by Frank as he set up his supplies. He was wrapping a bundle of sage with some kind of cordage and had a lighter at the ready.

I walked right past him, got in my car, and left without looking back.

CHAPTER EIGHT

I CONTINUED TO MY classes the next couple of days. Luckily, everyone else had moved on and forgotten that anything had been interesting about me last week. We had our Monday night seminar on students with special needs and the laws to protect them. I knew we were discussing the difference between modifying curriculum and making accommodations for students with emotional needs, but I wasn't paying any attention, despite this being the one class that Josephine taught personally. The head of the program, and I was blatantly ignoring the class discourse.

I never used to open my laptop during class. I knew it gave the impression (which was honestly the reality) that you weren't paying attention to the lecture, and I wanted to be perceived as an attentive listener. I took my notes in a notebook with my pen. Not that I ever looked back at my notes—these classes weren't the type you had tests in, just major projects and essays.

Anyway, it was that Monday that I first opened my laptop in the presence of a professor. I sat on the periphery of the room again, with my face on my computer screen during most of the two hours that passed. I didn't even try to school my features into an expression that looked interested, or even content. I let myself be. Without the mask of polite attentiveness and appreciation—the nice, good, sweet girl I always had to be. I let myself *be*.

The only time during class that my attention was piqued was when Ivy engaged in an aside conversation with Josephine personally. Josephine had taken a side tangent about using appropriate and inclusive language to describe students with disabilities, when Ivy piped up about the inappropriate language she hears from her high school students.

"I hear the most *oppressive* words coming from their mouths, and I am disturbed at how carelessly they can throw them out without consideration. How can I address this in a way that is calling students in rather than calling them out?"

That was Ivy's catchphrase—calling "in" rather than calling "out" something you see that isn't politically correct. She'd done this once to me during fall term—it still burned in my mind with the bright, unforgettable flame that only shame could produce.

We'd been put in a group to read an excerpt of *Pedagogy of the Oppressed* by Paulo Freire, a staple piece of literature in teacher school. Freire was Brazilian. I don't speak Portuguese, and I was one of many of us who kept mispronouncing his name. Fray-ruh? Free-ray? For the life of me, I thought I'd never get it right.

Apparently, that was the wrong opinion to express to Ivy.

She was explaining something that she'd gleaned from the reading and taking way too long for my patience, stumbling over pronouncing Freire, so I said, "Oh, whatever, it doesn't matter. We all know who you mean!" I waved my hand dismissively and smiled.

I was trying to lighten the tension in her voice, let her know that it didn't matter to us, that she should get to her point instead of worrying about the author's name.

Well, it did matter. And I'm an awful person for saying it didn't.

"It does matter!" she snapped back, raising her hands up in

frustration. "He was an oppressed person, and it matters that we remember his name correctly!"

Well, I felt like shit.

But I felt worse after I jumped into this conversation with Ivy and Josephine.

"I totally agree." I spoke up, my voice a little crusty from not using it for the last few hours. "I hear the most outrageous language coming out of my students every day."

Ivy looked appreciatively at me, like she had an ally. It felt good. Ivy never seemed to consider me on the same level as her. She looked between me and Josephine, tossing her head of beautiful, bouncy blond curls.

"What sorts of words are you hearing?" Josephine asked as she took a seat at Ivy's table, next to mine. I had to lean over to be in the conversation. Ivy was about to continue, but I was excited to be included, so I went first.

"I hear a lot of slurs, like the R-word, the F-slur, things like that that I haven't heard in years."

Ivy nodded and jumped in. "At my school, the socioeconomic status is a lot higher than the average, so I hear a lot of language referring to how they could get people of color arrested for threatening them when they didn't, or how they could afford to get out of a crime by paying the fees. How can I approach a conversation about this type of rhetoric with them?" She cocked her head slightly, like a puppy waiting for her treat. I imagined Josephine as a dog trainer, parading a tail-wagging Ivy around the showroom on a leash.

Josephine looked contemplative for a moment, then turned to me. "What you're talking about—that's just middle-schooler stuff. That's nothing new." She turned back to Ivy, pointing at her with her entire hand. "That's a real problem. Tell me more about the students saying these things."

And with that, I was expelled from the conversation. Rest

assured, I would never try to engage in that kind of discourse again. I would keep my mouth shut, listening but not adding to the conversation.

I turned back to my laptop, looking at nothing in particular.

Maybe I was too tired from pretending all day at school, or maybe I just didn't care anymore, but I let my face tell anyone who bothered to look at me just how I felt. I didn't think anyone was looking my way until I looked up and made direct eye contact with Luke. Gazing at me again, or simply a coincidence?

I got my answer the next day during our Tuesday class on methods for teaching students whose first language isn't English.

English for Speakers of Other Languages, or ESOL, was taught by this really rank guy named Jared. A full-time middle school teacher, Jared taught this single class at the university purely for the prestige and to get out his frustrations on us. At least, that was my theory.

Jared was such an asshole that even though his assignments made no applicable sense to our lives, he refused to explain them further. He was impossible to reach via email—the only way to gain a conference with him was to get right up in his face, and you'd probably get spat on.

We all hated Jared, but we couldn't say we hated Jared. Jared was Jewish, part of an ethnic group that was historically oppressed, and everything about our program stated that in order to be social-justice-oriented, we had to support members of oppressed groups. So, I couldn't *say* that Jared was an asshole, but Jared was an asshole.

Anyway, Jared was going on about something related to racial profiling, but I wasn't listening because I was trying to look at Luke without really looking at Luke. I knew he was watching me, even though he appeared intent on whatever was on his laptop.

He clearly didn't have the same values I did when it came to being on your computer during class instructional time, but I didn't have room to judge because I had recently developed the same habit.

Luke was looking at his computer, but he was also stealing glances at me. And I was stealing glances at him, and Adam, between us, didn't seem to notice anything at all.

I had just about given up on trying to decipher his side glances when a notification binged on my computer screen. The noise wasn't too loud, but it pinged loudly enough to pull the attention of everyone near me and to warrant a nasty look from Jared.

I muted the sound on my computer, and if my cheeks hadn't already been red from the embarrassment of the pinging message, they would have warmed when I saw that the message was from Luke.

He'd messaged me from across the table! I looked up to see his reaction to the ping, but he wasn't looking at me. No, he was facing forward, apparently listening intently to Jared. But his face had a little tiny smile that assured me he knew I was looking at him.

I glanced back at the message: *Jared's fly is down. Pass it on.*

I didn't dare look at Jared for confirmation of this before I typed back: *Why are you looking, weirdo?*

His reply was almost instantaneous, but he didn't even look up at me from his computer, his face holding a small smirk. *I gotta get my money out of this godforsaken class I'm going into major debt to take.*

I didn't have a clever reply for that one. I was stumped, trying to think of something to say when he messaged again. *I like your hair that way.*

There it was: that hint of flirtation that didn't really count as flirtation. He was diplomatic that way. I knew he wouldn't show all his cards. Anything he said had to have multiple interpretations that could get him off the hook, should he need it. Not one to incriminate myself either, I knew I had to be strategic.

I looked up at him, caught his eye, and silently mouthed "*Thank you.*"

I was on the edge of my seat, waiting to see if this conversation would continue, when I was interrupted by Jared explaining our latest and greatest assignment.

"Each of you will be required to spend an hour observing or assisting in an English Language Development classroom. You will write a reflection paper about your experiences, synthesizing the pedagogy you see with the educational theory behind it. You must complete these observation hours and the assignment before our meeting next week."

He said the last part like a threat, as if any of us in this intensive program would dare miss a deadline.

"Ask the ELD teachers at your placement schools if you can shadow for a day this week. Let your primary cooperating teachers know that this is an important assignment for your program."

Great. Not only was this just another thing to add to my plate—but it was perhaps a greater challenge for me than a lot of people. Rocky Middle didn't offer ELD services.

I wasn't sure how that was legal, but that really wasn't my issue at the moment. My problem was going to be finding a completely different school that I could observe in. Again, I cursed my lack of connections. My only avenue was Jared, so I hung back after class to ask him.

I dreaded approaching him, if only because he was such an abrasive man, and he kind of smelled. I usually left class immediately to get home as soon as possible. It was 9 p.m., I needed to do homework and shower, and I had to walk home in the dark alone.

Because I never lingered after class, it felt extremely unnatural to loiter in the classroom until the chatter died down, with everyone exiting slowly. Luke was one of the lingering souls, making passing comments to a few people as he left. God, he was so schmoozy. Like, everything out of that guy's mouth was aimed at pleasing someone or making them like him. I'd always known that about Luke, though. He was a charmer.

He looked like he was about to make one of his comments toward me, probably about the look on my face when his message pinged, but at that moment the person that had been occupying Jared's attention bid their adieus and walked away. I seized the opportunity to gain his attention.

You know when you approach someone, and they already look annoyed with you before you open your mouth? That's how Jared looked at me: with such contempt and disturbance. At least he didn't pity me, I guess. Maybe he didn't know about what happened last week. After all, he was a full-time teacher in the Big Bend School District.

"Hi, Jared, about our observation assignment? The school I'm student teaching in doesn't offer any ELD classes—"

"Then find another school to observe in." He cut me off. What an ass. I was really trying here.

"Yeah, I know. I was hoping you might have a recommendation for a school I could observe in? Or contact info for a teacher you know? I don't know this town very well," I said as patiently as I could.

"I'd be willing to let you perform a few practicum hours in my classroom at Grant," he said. "You may come in next Monday for my morning sessions."

"Thank you, Jared, but the morning sessions won't work for me. That's when I have my student teaching." The asshat hadn't even asked my schedule before telling me when I would be coming to his room. He didn't say any of it like a question either. I guess he had the power here, though. "Do you have an afternoon class I could observe?"

"Be there by one p.m. on Monday. You can watch my advanced English learners."

That settled it then. I had to admit, I was a little curious to enter into one of the fanciest, newly built schools on that side of town and to see how Jared interacted with middle school students. The thought was a little frightening—and intriguing.

CHAPTER NINE

ROCKY MIDDLE SCHOOL was offering free massages. That was the big news when I arrived at school that morning, after parking in the visitor lot and pushing through the crowd of obese twelve-year-olds. We were back to having students wait outside, obviously.

Rocky had brought in masseuses for the day—for the staff. Although I wasn't part of the staff, I should participate, Mrs. Means said. I wasn't sure why she felt the need to make the distinction, but okay. I'd take a free massage.

Not while I needed to be teaching, though, to be clear. I was to attain my massage during Mrs. Means's prep period so that I was really earning my hours. She had laughed when she said that. I must have chuckled back, like you do when you're trying to be polite but really someone is grinding your gears.

I wandered down the hallways of the decrepit school to the conference room behind the main office, where this massage session would be held. I was a little apprehensive. I definitely had a personal space bubble that was limited, and I wasn't wild about strangers touching me. My concern vanished, however, when I stepped into the room and saw what was awaiting me.

There were no massage tables, no oils, no relaxing music or hot towels. I had only been to a spa once, with my grandma for my fourteenth birthday, but that was what I pictured when I was offered a massage. There were a few black wheely desk chairs brought in from the computer lab and a few semiprofessional-looking adults milling about. They perked up when I walked in, like I was the first customer in a very long retail day.

"Hi there!" the very obviously gay man said to me with an excited wave. "Massage time?" He was tall, at least six-foot-one. His hair was shaved on the sides while the top stuck nearly straight up. It was that teal color that hair turns when it was at some point dyed blue but has faded. His V-neck shirt was low enough to expose the slightest bit of chest hair.

"Um, yes please, sure," I said as I took a few steps into the room, toward the chair he was gesturing.

"Great, right here!" he said as I plopped down in the chair. It wasn't comfortable, but it was better than the wooden chair I usually sat in in Mrs. Means's room.

"So what's your name and what do you teach?" he said excitedly as he pushed my hair off my shoulders and began feeling the back of my neck.

I tried not to tense up, to relax into it, but I also cringed at the thought of small talk. If I had known it wasn't going to be a silent massage, I wouldn't have come.

His hands were cold, but his aura was warm.

"I'm Rachel, and I'm, um, a student teacher in social studies."

"*Oh*, social studies! I always loved history," the man said. "I'm Cole, and this is Danika." He was probably nodding toward his companion, though I couldn't see with my head facing down as he lightly rubbed the place where my neck met my shoulders. I knew he meant the dark-haired short woman who he'd been chatting with when I walked in.

The only other person who'd been getting a massage was getting up to leave. Though my hair was pushed in my face, I saw the shadow of her step out the door, leaving us as the only three in the room.

Why was I the only one taking up the free massage? Probably because it was two people standing behind office chairs, and we had a million things we could be working on instead of getting a half-assed massage, but Cole seemed nice and eager to chitchat, so I indulged him.

"So, why'd you want to get into teaching?" he asked.

"Well, I have always loved school. It was like my happy place," I said honestly. I wasn't usually in the business of opening up to strangers, but he seemed harmless. And I couldn't remember the last time someone asked me about myself in earnest.

"Oh my God, girl, I cannot relate," Danika said, chuckling. "But good for you! I wish I'd had a cool young teacher like you."

"Thanks," I said, smiling. "I guess it was just important to me to feel like I make a difference."

"Oh, you do for sure. I could *not* do what you do. I wouldn't have the patience," Danika said, almost exasperated. I always wondered if people actually meant things like that or if they just said them because they thought it made teachers feel important and unique.

"Sometimes I barely have the patience either," I said. "Sometimes I think these kids really need to grow up."

Cole moved his hands up the base of my skull. It actually felt really nice, if only just to be touched. Besides Lucie's hug on Friday, it was the first physical contact I'd had in months.

"Yeah, I get that, but also they're kids! I wish I'd been allowed to be more of a kid when I was one, you know what I mean?" Cole said.

Danika went off then, but I was in my own world, my mind racing. Why was I so eager for these students to grow up, when that's exactly how my childhood was?

I never got the chance to be a worry-free kid. I resented the adults in my life for it. And yet, I was frustrated because these students around me were doing just the thing I always thought they should be allowed to. My head hurt. Maybe I expected too much from my students.

I left the massage experience unsure if it made me feel better or worse.

CHAPTER TEN

I WAS BEING FORCED to socialize for Lucie's birthday. Under usual circumstances, I was fairly antisocial, but after the last week, I especially didn't want to be around a bunch of people. But Lucie was turning twenty-two, which apparently felt like a big deal. Besides, it would be our last birthday to celebrate while living together, she had reasoned.

I didn't remind her that my birthday was coming up in March, because I knew what she meant. We never celebrated my birthday. Not because I didn't like my birthday, but because my quiet, semi-antisocial behavior always seemed to leave the impression that I didn't want to be celebrated, and I never corrected anybody.

We were to go to a bar that had billiards so all of Lucie's friends could gather around her, tell her how amazing she was, and sing "22" by Taylor Swift. Not really my scene, but I'd do it for Lucie. I always did it for Lucie. Against my better judgment, time and time again, I'd go with her to the bars, to the dance clubs, to frat parties when we were younger. I hadn't been to a frat party since I was a sophomore, and I didn't intend to go to one any time soon.

Or ever again.

So I set off with Lucie and Amy to meet up with her colossal group of friends and pseudo-friends at The Pike, an off-campus bar that was kind of in the middle of nowhere. It wasn't usually populated with college students, since you needed a car to get there, and the University of Big Bend was notoriously so limited on parking that it cost a fortune to have a parking pass, so most students didn't have a car.

We took Amy's car so Lucie could get drunk off her ass, feeling loved and celebrated and cherished. It was times like these that I always wished I could feel the same excitement and genuine enthusiasm that these people seemed to show for going out and drinking and celebrating a friend. I always felt like I was faking it, pretending to be excited even though everyone could probably tell I was really a sourpuss. It was especially hard to put on that front today; I'd been wearing a mask of stability since last Friday.

We had dressed up in cute outfits, and Lucie's idea of cute meant dressing sexy. She felt you could only look good if you looked appealing to your desired sex. So, the night of her birthday, I had my boobs out. Not even tastefully. They were just hanging out of my low-cut shirt. Or hanging out as much as B-cups could, I guess. I'm not even sure why I still had the top, which surpliced so obviously across my chest. It was also cropped short, so even with my high-waisted pants, you could see the whole of my navel.

It was also still the heart of winter, so though it didn't get blisteringly cold in Big Bend, it was rainy and chilly. Oh well, the things you do in the name of sex appeal, I guess.

Despite the cleavage, I wasn't nearly the most underdressed of the group. This wasn't scandalous for Lucie and her friends—this was just their usual aesthetic. I felt uncomfortable, but I was willing to pretend for the night. It was a good distraction. That's what I kept trying to tell myself.

We entered the bar establishment, which was apparently famous for some C-list actor who had worked there in the 1970s, and found Lucie's cadre between two pool tables. Though I usually didn't like hanging out with people who weren't my close friends, it was kind of nice to be around people who didn't know me well. People who weren't in my program, who wouldn't talk to me about student teaching. People who didn't know where I'd been last Friday.

Though I wasn't a fan of small talk, I didn't mind it much that night. At least it didn't revolve around students, long essays, or gun violence. I didn't drink, partially because I never really drank and also because I still had to teach in the morning.

Most of Lucie's friends seemed to have scheduled their college classes in the afternoons and had all morning to sleep off whatever they consumed. There were only a dozen or so people gathered around our tables, most of whom I knew, except the few underclassmen who had been added to the entourage sometime in the last few months. I'd been drowning in schoolwork and hadn't come out much. The majority were seniors, or at least fourth-year students. A few I knew wouldn't finish their degree for at least a few more terms. Milking it, I suppose. That time in life when your only responsibility is to be a student, a time when you can stay out until 3 a.m. on a Wednesday because you don't have to be up until noon.

Maybe if I was smart, I would have pushed back the responsibility too.

Lucie herself had stated on multiple occasions that since this was her last year of college, she just wanted to have *fun*. She just wanted to enjoy her last hurrah as a young adult without a real job, without a family to support, living the college lifestyle to the fullest. *Fun.*

Every time she gave me the speech, I had the same feeling that she was trying to convince me to do the same, knowing very well that, with this internship-like schedule of student teaching and night classes, I had no time for *fun*. Not to mention that our ideas of fun were clearly polar opposites, present situation included.

So I sat with my glass of Pepsi, lying by omission every time someone assumed it was a rum and Coke. Just as well. If they knew I wasn't drinking, they would push me to drink. It had been the same story for as long as I could remember. I never really enjoyed alcohol, not only because I suffered from major motion sickness while completely sober and didn't particularly enjoy feeling dizzy, but because I didn't enjoy the taste. I never admitted this to anybody, but I didn't enjoy feeling unaware in public. It felt unsafe to be out of my mind. So I pretended and smiled, changing the subject every time anyone asked what I was drinking.

August, one of Lucie's periphery friends I had only met a couple of times, settled on a barstool next to me and seemed keen to strike up a conversation. August was always pleasant enough, if not a little overbearing. Not in an abrasive way, but more like a dog—she was loveable but obnoxious. She always seemed like she was panting and would jump on you if she got excited. Definite golden-retriever energy. It matched with her long, wavy, golden hair.

So Golden August sat next to me, beer in hand, clearly slightly intoxicated, and started telling me (panting) about her work on the Big Bend University newspaper. Right, she was studying journalism. Kind of a cop-out major, if you ask me. So few people who got a degree in journalism actually went on to do anything with it. It was just a degree that was somewhat applicable to lots of fields, and the classes were easy. Like, seriously, someone who takes "Media Studies" class gets the same bachelor's degree as someone who took organic chemistry? Cop-out.

I wasn't sure if August was going anywhere with the topic, until she said, "So Rachel, you're student teaching at Rocky Middle, right? You were there for that shooting last week? I'm doing a story on it for the paper, and Lucie told me you'd know about it. It'd be super cool if I could interview you about it!"

I would have hoped that my face didn't betray how stunned I was, if I could think of anything but how stunned I was.

Lucie was advertising to people what I had been through? I thought Lucie had more tact than that—that she could see that I didn't want to talk about it, and the fewer people that knew, the better.

I'd thought Lucie was empathetic. I thought this August girl could be empathetic, if she was going to use her journalistic skills to discuss current events with strangers. I was trying to formulate a response, August still staring at me eagerly, when Lucie approached, only slightly drunk. She slung an arm around me. "August and Rachel and everyone, all here together for my B-day! Happy birthday to me!" She sang out.

August must have felt the need for reinforcements because she tried again to come for my throat, this time using Lucie as her modem. "Lucie, I was just telling Rach it would be *so* cool if she could tell me about her experience in the school shooting for the article I'm writing. So far, no news source in town has gotten an actual witness. She could literally be the first one."

I felt Lucie tense slightly, but she didn't say anything. She looked at me, then back to August, then to the drink in her right hand. She slugged back what was left of her foamy beer, let out a burp, giggled, and said, "Come on, August, don't be Miss Journalism Queen tonight. Get drunk with me for my party!" She dropped her arm from around me and grabbed August's hand. Really, I knew it wasn't an affront to me, but it felt like she had just taken August's side in this war. She walked away with August, off to order another pitcher, probably.

I started shaking. I was shivering so violently that I was worried I might be going hypothermic. My tiny top didn't help. Was it cold in here? Was the air-conditioning on at night in late January? I needed to get out of here. I needed to go home.

Amy had driven us. I should have known I would regret not driving myself, especially since I was the one not drinking, but I'd rather find my own way home than have to be responsible for getting all the drunk people home in my car. Especially since they would likely be out way later than I wanted to be.

I didn't bother trying to face Lucie, who would pressure me into staying and having a real drink. Instead, I chose Amy, talking to a group of tall, athletic-looking girls. I interrupted, not caring if it looked rude.

"Hey, Amy, I'm going to take off." Sweet and short. No excuse needed. I'd always been a fan of the "Irish goodbye," where you simply leave a party without saying anything, but I didn't want anyone worrying about where I'd gone. If anyone would notice anyway.

I was kind of surprised that Amy diverted her attention away from the pretty girls long enough to argue with me.

"What? No, we just got here!" she whined, but I didn't back down. I didn't say any more. I just started backing away.

"Do you need me to take you?" she said with a look on her face like she was silently begging me to say no. At least she was offering, even if it was insincere.

"Oh no, no, you stay. I'll find my way home. Don't worry."

I knew she wouldn't worry. No one would. So I didn't bother with any more goodbyes. I took off, out the door, without so much as wishing the birthday girl well.

CHAPTER ELEVEN

I PROBABLY WOULD HAVE walked all the way if it hadn't been for the shivering. I took off on foot, keeping to streetlamp lit sidewalks. I only made it a few blocks before I did the smarter thing and called for a ride. I might be flighty, but I still had decent judgment when it came to safety.

I didn't really have many friends outside of Lucie and her friends, and I wasn't close enough with anyone in my cohort to ask them for a favor like this. The thought actually passed through my pathetic brain to call Mrs. Means, if only because she was a responsible adult with a car and I had her phone number.

In the end, I called a cab. I didn't have the Uber app—I'd never needed it. I wasn't about to download it now while shivering on a street corner in the middle of nowhere. So I'd gone the old-fashioned way and literally looked up the phone number for a taxi. The cab company said they'd be there within fifteen minutes. I had to stay put.

My feelings caught up with me now that I was alone. I slowly sat down on the cold concrete, the damp humidity sinking into my bones, making my chill more severe. Was it really that cold, or was I getting a fever or something?

Tears had burned my eyes since I walked out of The Pike, but it was only now that a sob escaped my lips. I tried to clamp down on it. I took a shaky breath. Then I let loose. Sobs racked through me as I sat on the dirty sidewalk, waiting for my overpriced cab to take me home.

***

I was called out of Mrs. Means's class halfway into first period. The first half of the period, I was busy escorting Charles down to the office and back so he could get dry pants. The little bastard didn't even say anything this time—usually, he would let someone know that he had wet himself. That morning, he sat there silently until I stepped in the puddle of his urine that had accumulated next to his seat. Later I would have to scrub the bottom of my Mary Janes. Ugh.

When I got back from the office with a dry Charles, a woman I hadn't seen before was waiting by the door.

"Ms. Harding?" she asked as I sent Charles in the room, pausing at the threshold myself. Alarm bells went off in my head as someone in this school addressed me by my full last name.

Mrs. Means still only called me "Miss H," and I wasn't entirely sure she knew my full last name. My heart picked up in tempo as I put on my "nice, responsible, respectable adult" face. "Yes?"

"I'm Amanda Jones, and I'm an attorney for the school district. Will you please come with me for a few minutes? I just need to talk to you briefly." She gestured across the hallway to an abandoned classroom that was used for storage. It was probably where ELD classes were held, once upon a time. I didn't say anything as I followed her across the hall.

A step behind her, my mind raced with everything I could have done wrong. I'd tried so hard to fill the role expected of me—what had I done? Was I being let go? Where else could I complete my student-teaching hours? Did I say something that put a target on me for being callous? Was it my yellow sweater on Monday?

My thoughts were venturing into panic mode as we sat at the only available chairs in the room: an older desk chair with the fake leather flaking off and a child's chair. She, of course, sat in the adult-sized chair, leaving me across from her, looking the part of a small, scared, isolated child.

"We already spoke to the rest of the staff at the end of the day last Friday," she began, "but you had already left. I'm required to touch base with you about the process of what happens next and what we will need from you, okay?"

She spoke to me like I was a kid. Maybe I looked like one, with how freaked out I felt. Still, I nodded and put on my best brave face.

"Yes, please tell me what you'll need from me." I tried to sound sincere. She appeared to buy it as she went on. She was very to-the-point; clearly, she had places to be.

"First of all, the district's official statement about the incident stands that this was a case of self-defense, and defense in the name of the students and staff here, but the case is above the discernment of any local courts—it's going to the attorney general. The school resource officer is on leave until the case is settled. The child of the deceased will be back at school here when he is ready. What questions do you have?"

I didn't want to seem dense, but I also did have questions. So, so many questions—most of which probably weren't appropriate for this woman. So, I asked, "What will the court decide? What will the outcome be?"

Her face pulled in a way that told me she didn't have the perfect answer to that particular question, like she was frustrated that I asked it. It made me feel incredibly young. And naive.

"I really can't speculate," she said diplomatically, "but I do know that, with a controversial case such as this, there is likely to be pushback from the public, regardless of the verdict."

When I didn't interrupt, she went on. "What the district is gathering is evidence from the time of the event. We need to collect all the information of the people who were here. Or, rather, the adults who were present. We are going to need to get a copy of all your text messages, emails, and any other communication records from Friday while you were at the school. You'll get your phone back in a few minutes. We just need to connect it to our computer to download your information."

I nodded, my heart pounding and my stomach in knots at the idea of the police searching my phone record, my texts. *I hope I didn't say anything too embarrassing.*

"May I ask any questions of you, about the case? I would like to clear things up for my own conscience," I asked with trepidation. Usually, I wouldn't ask if I thought the answer would be no, but I didn't have anything to lose. My pride was already gone, as I was sitting in a child's chair and was about to hand over my phone.

She stared back at me evenly. "Again, I won't be able to speculate, but I can clarify facts for you."

I took a breath and held her gaze. "I know that this case will be . . . controversial . . . possibly highly publicized . . . because it was a police-involved incident?" I couldn't bring myself to say the words "shooting" or "death" or "murder."

I continued, "And because it includes a queer person of color . . . but is there evidence to signify that they were intending to cause more harm than they did?"

Again, Miss Lawyer Lady seemed uncomfortable or unsure of how to answer the question. The fact that she'd dropped her professional poker face made me feel only slightly better—more confident that she was being transparent with me. She neither nodded nor shook her head. She was steady.

"That's why the . . . *incident* . . . is under heavy scrutiny and investigation," she replied. "You'll know as soon as I do, as soon as the state attorney general releases it."

I nodded. I guess I'd have to accept that that's all I would get for now.

"Thank you for answering my questions," I said as I stood from the toddler-sized chair. "I'll go get my phone."

I went quietly across the hall to retrieve my phone from its home under the desk.

When I handed it to Ms. Jones, I felt sick. I didn't say anything as I returned to class.

It was brought back to me by an office aide fifteen minutes later. Everything on it looked exactly the same; it just felt wrong knowing that all of my data and information had been copied onto someone else's computer.

But again, that was all the peace I was going to get for now. Maybe I had to get accustomed to not feeling at peace.

CHAPTER TWELVE

I DIDN'T HAVE CLASS again until Friday evening, when I had to return to my methods class with the beloved Annabel.

I really couldn't even relay what topics of importance we talked about in Annabel's class. All we seemed to have were self-serving discussions about how very politically correct we all were. I didn't engage; I hardly even listened.

Annabel had been instructing us to evaluate our own cultural and racial biases, as if we hadn't been doing that from the first day we were admitted to this program. Literally, part of our application included an essay portion where we explained what being a culturally revitalizing teacher meant to us. If we made it past that stage, we were invited for an interview with the program administrators.

It was a group interview. Mine had four other applicants in it, including Adam and Luke. The other two didn't make it into the program, apparently. I remember meeting those two guys that day, nervously waiting in the hallway outside the room where the interviews were to be held—the exact room I was seated in now, actually. When there's only one education building on campus, you tend to spend a lot of time in the same couple of rooms.

It was odd to think about how different things had felt then—how much I had changed since last winter. Thinking about myself a year ago, I felt a weird mixture of emotions—pity, for how little she knew, and something else, maybe envy—also for how little she knew.

I was the first one to arrive at the interview. I had scheduled it early in the week, as I was always keen to be early. My logic was that if I chose a time slot toward the beginning of the week, I had a better chance of getting in. If I waited until the end of the week, maybe they would have had a plethora of decent interviews and already filled the available spots.

I was looking down, smoothing my new dress, when Luke walked in. It wasn't a *new* new dress, but it was new to me. I didn't have a car yet, so I had begged Lucie to take me shopping. I didn't actually have to beg that hard, because Lucie was always down for a shopping trip. Plus, I promised to fill her gas tank for taking me. Still, I couldn't afford much, so she took me to Goodwill.

There, we'd scavenged for the perfect interview outfit: one that made me look professional and mature, while also making me feel confident and cute. We'd settled on a LOFT dress with a broken zipper that I could cover with a light sweater. I couldn't find a sweater the right color, but Lucie had one at home that I could borrow.

The dress was black with light green flowers. It had a high neck that gave it a modest look, and it went almost down to my knees. It kind of made me look like a middle-aged mom, especially with my hair back in a low ponytail, but I guess that was the vibe I was going for. Complete with Lucie's light green cardigan, I was ready to be accepted into the program.

I was nervously smoothing it down when a tall man walked in. My first thought was that he had to be joining my group for the interview, given his attire and timing. My second thought was how attractive he was. He walked with the air of someone who knew how handsome he was. He was tall, but he leaned forward on his feet like he didn't need the height to make his presence known. He wore black corduroy pants that were fitted, a button-down shirt with a tie, and a rain jacket. I hadn't bothered with a rain jacket; it would ruin my look.

His dark curly hair was offset by his hazel eyes. It was hard to tell behind his glasses, but they were definitely somewhere between a light caramel brown and a forest green. Maybe it depended on the light?

It had definitely sunken in how cute he was when I came to my senses and remembered why I couldn't be distracted with these thoughts right now: For one, I needed to be on my A game for this interview, and two, I was vehemently against starting up a romantic entanglement with someone in Big Bend. In one year, I would be graduating and cultivating my dream life someplace else. A place that felt more *me*.

Luckily, I didn't have to worry about making a fool of myself in front of this guy for long, because before either of us spoke, Adam walked in the door behind him.

Adam was the opposite of Luke: short, with a buzzcut, likely to hide the fact that he was balding, and I had no sultry thoughts about him. Not then, not ever.

The perfect dousing of cold water to keep my brain focused.

We all semisheepishly (except Luke—nothing was ever sheepish about Luke) introduced ourselves, our other two companions joining moments before we were all ushered into the room to sit around a table and answer questions.

The questions were all social-justice-oriented. We had mere moments to formulate a response before reporting back in front of the others. I was honestly proud of myself for how I kept from getting flustered. I also knew how I was supposed to feel about all the issues at hand—racism bad, advocating for minorities good. Equality bad, equity good. It was imperative that we could explain the difference at a moment's notice.

Lucie had helped coach me, drilling me with her own political agenda. Lucie was extremely politically inclined and insisted that everyone around her be as well. It was usually a little annoying, but today I was grateful. All of her prodding about posting on social media about every injustice, rallying people to go to demonstrations, and quizzing people about equitable policies was about to pay off.

In fact, that was the first interview question.

"Do you think it is more important in education to focus on the equality of all students or building equitable conditions for all?"

They came to me first, as I sat nearest the front of the room, closest to the interrogators.

"I know, even more than I believe, that it is vital to achieve equitable conditions in schools. Equality is a strategy to provide all with the same thing, ignoring the nuances necessary to meet the needs of individuals. To be equitable means to provide to each what *they* need, which must differ from person to person, by definition."

I got an approving nod from Luke before they moved onto his response next.

The rest of the questions were relevant to the themes we covered throughout the year of student teaching. Things like how to support students in diverse circumstances, connect with families, and differentiate curriculum. Questions like "Students at your school are establishing a Black Student Union. Some White students feel left out and come to you requesting support in establishing a White Student Union. What language do you use to explain to them your position on this?"

It all felt like a big test before we'd even begun the program. A test to see if we could be shaped into their mold of inclusive, modern educators.

A test that Ivy always had the right answers for. She bought into all of this more than anyone I knew. We all preached it. I just wondered how many actually used all of it frequently in their classrooms. I tried, I really did, but I just felt like I couldn't institute any of it until I had more of a voice in my own classroom.

That Friday in Annabel's class, Ivy was having what appeared to be a one-on-one conversation with Annabel in front of the class. Specifically, she was showing our professor her engagement ring, Annabel cooing accordingly.

All Ivy talked about was her engagement. All any engaged girls talked about was their engagement. I wondered if I'd be the same someday. If I was lucky enough to find someone that I'd be that proud of marrying, would I brag to anyone who would listen? Most women seemed that way, though I had to wonder if it was always about the *perfect* guy or the fact that, historically, women getting married raised their social status.

With Ivy, it seemed to be both, but also the fact that she was marrying outside her race. I know; that seems ridiculous to be notable in the twenty-first century, but in a cohort that was constantly discussing these racial and social-justice-oriented issues, any talking point that made you seem less White was a point of honor.

I didn't have any of these. I was whitey-white-white, and my only strategy in talking about it was trying to be upfront about the fact that I had no oppression to fall back on. Some of the women seemed keen on using their sex to their advantage, consistently giving presentations on women's rights or struggles. Likewise, some of the men had no choice but to play up the socioeconomic role, talking about gentrification in neighborhoods and underprivileged students.

Lucie was always like that too—ethnically, as plain as white bread—but she had been blessed by some goddess as looking like the most racially ambiguous person you'd ever seen. Her shiny long hair was as black as hair can be, her eyes were a rich dark brown, and her skin tanned beautifully in the warm months. She was beautiful, and people were constantly asking her where she was from. They'd never believe her when her voice would get high-pitched as she'd giggle and say she was Russian.

Ivy, however, despite being as White as me, down to the light-toned hair and blue eyes, got bonus points for marrying a Latino man. They'd been high school sweethearts. Apparently, this was winning an approving look from Annabel, as Ivy showed the professor her ring and was explaining the prejudice against mixed race couples she faced regularly. Annabel was very apt to talking about this because she was in an interracial marriage as well. Annabel was married to a wonderful Black man, apparently, and had three beautiful children. Isn't that nice. What was I paying for this class again?

Ivy was gushing about how excited she was to bear the last name Pinedo once she married, and how grateful she was to be accepted into Carlos's family, when Luke snorted softly across from me. Adam gave him a knowing look, both of them keeping their heads low.

"I know, right?" Adam said under his breath.

"Shh." Luke smiled. "Shut up!"

"What?" I asked, genuinely curious for being left out of what was obviously some private joke.

Adam looked like he maybe would have told me, if Luke didn't lean across the table at me to say, "I'll tell you later."

I could accept later.

I went back to not paying attention to the discussion at hand when a notification blared silently across my computer screen. I'd had the sense to mute it after Tuesday's fiasco in Jared's class, just in case.

Of course, it was Luke texting me across the table. I was hoping he was telling me about the private joke, but even better, he was asking if I wanted to grab a slice of pizza after class. Just off campus, there was a pizza place where you could get a slice of cheap pizza with your Jell-O shots. They made good money from the Big Bend students.

I didn't hesitate before messaging that I was up for it. Those guys didn't invite me to do things very often, and I was excited to be included. I didn't always have much to say to them, especially since they were such *boys*. But hey, comrades were comrades, and one of them made my cheeks blush.

Luke didn't think of me that way—I knew that. None of them thought of me that way, and I knew why. It was my own fault, really. My program had multiple attractive, intelligent men, and yet I was as single as could be.

I'd like to think that I had intentionally made myself unavailable to the men in my program, for the sake of staying focused and planning a future outside of Big Bend, but it could also have to do with my demeanor. I was quiet, and not conventionally attractive, and I wasn't accessible to them, exactly like I hadn't been accessible to potential friends at the start of college.

Despite recognizing my shortcomings, I also had this weird sense that most people weren't worth my time. Was it a superiority complex? Maybe. But I couldn't stop myself from feeling better than the people around me, but also that I envied them for who they were. They seemed to have an easier time living in the world they were born into. I couldn't wait for the day that I felt settled, comfortable, and confident in my own life.

Really, I didn't have time for romance anyway. I couldn't make time for it right now. Maybe when I had my degree and my teaching license. Besides, I wanted a real, long-lasting relationship, and with this intensive program, I didn't have the time to deal with college tomfoolery.

When Annabel and Ivy had finished their conversation, Annabel seemed utterly bored with the class and dismissed us early. I stood up to gather my bag and coat when Adam surprised me by asking, "What are you guys doing tonight?" and Luke surprised me more by quickly saying, "Laundry. Sleeping. Otherwise being boring," giving me a conspirator's wink on the side that Adam couldn't see.

I'd never been a good liar, but if Luke wanted to be alone with me, I was going to go along with it. "Um, yeah. Just catching up on stuff. You?" I deflected.

I didn't hear his answer as I followed Luke into the dark rain outside.

CHAPTER THIRTEEN

WE WALKED THE three blocks to Rodeo's Pizza in relative silence, both our hoods up. We passed by a few groups of girls on their way to the bar. That was a weird side effect of having class late on Fridays—the world of college campuses was just coming alive when we were ready to drag our tired asses to bed. Or I was, at least.

I knew Luke was less of a homebody than I was—less quiet, less self-contained. I'd observed enough during our classes to know that though Luke held an incredibly cool exterior, he reacted strongly to things.

He certainly cared about his image and wanted people to like him. I could easily tell that much by the way he schmoozed with everyone, from compliments to feigned interest in whatever they were saying, genuine or not. Luke knew how to make people invested in him. He liked to be the center of attention.

It was that thought that made me break the silence to ask him, "Are you the youngest kid in your family?"

He paused as he opened the door to Rodeo's, giving me an

incredulous look as he held the door open, raising his arm above my head so I could be guided underneath him into the restaurant.

He still hadn't answered as I stepped into the line at the counter. The top floor of the pizza joint had a rather relaxed vibe. You ordered pizza by the slice from the counter, took a number, and waited at your table for it to be brought over.

There were wooden booths set up along both walls, with a few small tables in the middle that I had never seen occupied. There were a few arcade games by the front door that always seemed to be out of order, and the few old TVs played sports games or old sitcom reruns, but it was my kind of place.

It was comfortable to come into the warmth after walking through the perpetual rain of the valley that Big Bend was housed in, and the wooden tones of everything from the ceilings to the benches and floor made it feel almost like a cabin.

The downstairs was where the debauchery happened. Underneath the main floor restaurant was the bar. It wasn't a wild bar, with dark lighting and dancing, like most of the campus dives, but it had the vibe of a speakeasy. I'd only been down to the bar once, with Lucie and her friends. They'd shot some pool and drank mixed liquor while I sat quietly drinking my Pepsi.

I was halfway worried that Luke would want to head to the basement, but when he ordered a draft beer from the counter, I figured I was in the clear. I hung back while he ordered two slices of pizza (the supreme kind with everything on it—if I was analyzing his pizza choice, which I totally wasn't, it might signify that he was adult enough not to be picky) and a tall craft IPA from a local brewery that sounded somewhat familiar.

He completed his order and turned back to me, not saying anything, but his expression danced with the question, *Do you want me to get yours?*

"I'll get mine," I said, sidestepping by him up to the counter. He didn't argue as he pulled out a debit card and paid while I ordered my single slice of pepperoni and a fountain Pepsi. I was hoping that if he was reading into my order, it read more like "classic tastes" than "little kid." He didn't say anything, though, as we took our drinks and our numbers and headed for a booth on the far side of the room.

"How'd you know I'm the youngest child?" he asked, finally responding to my earlier question.

"Please, you are a textbook younger child. You have baby energy. It's okay. I'm technically the youngest myself. That's why I can read it so well."

"What do you mean 'technically'?" he asked, his face wary.

"Well, I have older siblings. I just never really got to know them. They're a lot older than me and grew up in a totally different household. I was mostly raised by my grandma."

"So, really, you have more, like, only-child energy?" he said with a smirk. My eyes were drawn to the perfect peachy-pink shade of his lips.

"Yeah, I guess that's right," I said quietly.

"So, no beer?" he asked. I searched his eyes for the correct answer—what would seem the best to him? That I don't like beer, that I'm watching my figure, that I don't drink? I settled for a white lie.

"Didn't sound good. I'm a big fan of soda pop."

"Soda pop? Where are you from that you call it soda pop? This is the West Coast. Everyone calls it soda."

"Growing up, I heard so much argument over whether it was soda or pop, so I just combined the two. Soda pop sounds kind of vintage, don't you think?"

I wasn't sure why I always felt like I was on trial with him, like I had to say the right thing or he would lose interest in the conversation immediately. We were quiet for a beat long enough to hear the song softly playing from the speaker above our heads.

"Blegh, I hate this song," I said.

He recoiled. "You don't like Tame Impala?"

"No, I mean, I like Tame Impala just fine. I'm just tired of this song. My roommate used to overplay it way too much. She'd blast it."

"Big fan of Tame Impala, or what?"

I hesitated before answering.

"No... it's just. Well, she would play it super loudly and frequently when she and her girlfriend were, you know, getting frisky."

He laughed, and I'm not sure if it was what I said or the face I made while I said it.

"So it's her sex song?" he asked.

"Yeah, it was her sex song. For months!"

It felt good to be smiling. It felt natural. Our pizza was dropped off, and I watched as he immediately sprinkled red pepper flakes over the top. I was about to comment on it, or ask if he really liked spice, when he looked up like he was about to say something.

"So, earlier, when Ivy was going on and on and Adam laughed?"

Ahh, we were getting to that. I was pleased that he remembered to include me in whatever the inside joke was. It felt good to be part of the friend group, even if he'd excluded Adam from whatever this pizza outing was.

He took a large pull of his foamy beer before going on. I took his second of silence to speak.

"Not a fan of hearing all about her perfect wedding that she's having the week after graduation in June?" I asked innocently.

He exhaled briskly, with a small smile on his lips. "I would be, if I didn't know the truth about it."

Oh, this was serious gossip then. I looked at him expectantly. He looked me dead in the eyes and took a deep breath, like he was readying himself. His lips were quirked in the slightest smirk. He raised his eyebrows once quickly while he said, "I slept with Ivy."

I didn't let my surprise show. Weirdly, I felt a tinge of pain in my chest as it sunk in. How had he slept with Ivy? She'd bragged about how she and her betrothed had been together since they were fourteen.

"When?" is all I asked, feigning as much disinterest as I could muster.

He couldn't have been very ashamed, because he didn't hesitate before continuing his story.

"September, right after the program began. I guess she'd been fighting with her boyfriend, and we slept together a couple of times. Her apartment is, like, freakishly clean. So organized."

I'd hate for him to see my bedroom, if organization was a turnoff for him. I tried to push the thought from my mind.

"She broke it off, though, and now all she ever talks about is her Prince Charming and the dream wedding," he said, seeming to be done with his tale.

He'd had sex with Ivy at the house she shared with her fiancé. None of his story even seemed to be concerned with the fact that she'd been engaged at that time. But I wasn't about to hound him about morals.

Did her fiancé know? Who else knew? How many times did it happen? Did Luke really like her? Was he heartbroken? The curious side of me was dying to know more about the logistics of the situation, but I really just wanted to know more about Luke and his feelings about it.

"Geez, Luke. Are you the only ones in the cohort who have hooked up? Or are you trying to rack up your numbers?" I wasn't sure why I asked. Maybe because he was in the telling mood; maybe because I felt like I had to know who else he'd looked at before me. He wasn't too shy to tell me.

"You know Harper in the elementary cohort? I got her number, and we talked a bit, but we never hung out." I made a disgusted face that made him add, "You asked!"

"So, what now?" I asked. "Ivy is engaged, and Harper is otherwise inclined, and what about you?"

"Look, degree is numero uno right now, you know? Gotta get this teaching degree so I can pay off some of these outstanding student loans."

A nonanswer as far as his love life. I didn't know what bothered me more—that I didn't know or that I cared. I didn't want to care about who Luke liked. Luke was too cool of a guy to ever be with me anyway. He wasn't flirting with me; this wasn't a date. We were two cohort friends getting pizza and beer after class.

Why didn't he want Adam to come? A voice in the back of my head wagered, *Did he want to be alone with me?*

I didn't want to read too much into it. I didn't want to be one of those delusional people who made up relationships in their heads. I would have to take him at face value, no matter what. I vowed right then to take him at his word.

We finished our pizza, chitchatting about cohort members, the intramural sports he used to play, always scoring the winning goals—it definitely reinforced my ideas about him being constantly starved for attention. He told me about his student-teaching placement, and I didn't say much about mine. We bused our table, talking all the while, and put our hoods back up to head outside.

The cold had my teeth chattering, but I was still trying to maintain a conversation with Luke as we started off in the direction of my home, which happened to be the same direction of his. We discovered that he lived about four blocks west of me.

"I'll walk you home," he said, not really asking. My heart skipped a beat at the thought that he was being protective of me, and honestly, I wasn't ready to say goodbye yet.

We fell silent as we walked under the streetlamps. I found that, with Luke, saying nothing was better than prattling on about something unimportant. He seemed easily bored.

As we neared the corner where we would part, he didn't seem inclined to let me continue down the dark alleyway full of half-drunk frat boys alone. He walked me all the way to my front step. I turned around as I opened my front door, waiting for him to say something else—something to end this evening pleasantly.

"See you," he said as he turned to walk back down the alley. I watched him for only a few seconds before I shut and locked the door tightly behind me.

You never really knew where you stood with Luke.

CHAPTER FOURTEEN

I HAD RESIGNED MYSELF to work on lesson plans and homework over the weekend in between marathoning old episodes of *Sex and the City*. We didn't have much for a living room in our small apartment, so I pretty much lived in my bedroom.

Lucie had gotten the bigger room, and the room with the better view. Hers overlooked the small patch of grass and trees that our townhouse complex deemed a backyard, while my window faced the air shaft, meaning my view was about six feet of space before the neighbor's bedroom window.

It didn't matter much what my view looked like, anyway, because I mostly lived on my bed. In addition to sleeping, my bed was my primary location for schoolwork, eating, lounging, and organizing.

Lucie and I were also opposites when it came to organization. I really was neat, though I hadn't told Luke that. I kept my room extremely orderly, from the books on my shelf to the clothes in my closet, and I kept the rest of our small house clean too.

We didn't have very many dishes, so I saw to it that they all stayed cleaned and put away. Lucie had no such reservations. I regularly cleaned our shower, toilet, and other shared spaces. Lucie didn't seem fazed if things were dirty. Over time I realized that she just didn't notice, and maybe that was because she hadn't grown up cleaning up after herself like I had. Just like when I was young, I knew that if I didn't clean, I would be living in filth. And I just couldn't have that. So I became self-sufficient.

It was mid-Saturday afternoon, and I was, of course, on my bed. I had my computer open so I could tell myself I was working on homework, but really, I was looking at job postings to see if any teacher jobs were available yet. There weren't any, but it was still early.

Teaching is such a seasonal, cyclical line of work. That's something I actually liked about it—I liked the beginnings and ends, that each year had an end date and we would start anew the next fall.

Unfortunately for my current state of mind, it also meant that job postings all happened around the same time of year—late spring. Teacher's contracts were either renewed or terminated around April, and that was when jobs were posted and filled. If you didn't succeed in nailing down a contract by June, you'd have to gamble that somebody would quit by August and try to pick up a job before the school year began.

It was dicey, and I was absolutely not going to allow myself to be in that position—frankly, I couldn't afford to take that risk.

As soon as graduation day passed, Lucie and I would be moving out of this apartment, and I'd be moving to whatever location I could secure a job in. I planned to stay in the state, but other than that, I was fairly open.

I was sure I didn't want to move back to my hometown. I had left that far behind me as soon as I turned eighteen, graduated from high school, and zipped out to Big Bend. I'd always dreamed of going to a bigger school, in a bigger town, and that's exactly what Big Bend was.

Corning, where I grew up, was by no definition big. I wouldn't call it a small town, because that always evoked images of a *really* small town, with a single strip of local downtown shops and no fast-food chains. Corning was more medium-sized, though it didn't have much going for it. And I didn't even have friends or family to go back to there. Except for Grandma, though she now spent most of her time in Arizona.

No, I wouldn't be moving back to Corning. My sights were set on somewhere on the west side of the state, somewhere where I could afford the rent and have access to all the good stores once I was making real money.

Present job search over, I closed my laptop and pushed it aside, letting it take its place at the foot of my bed while I lounged back. It felt good to rest for a while. I had just closed my eyes to doze when my phone started vibrating. A call. No one ever called me, not even Grandma.

I picked it up, and my heart started racing when I saw who it was. I answered with no hesitation.

"Hello?"

"There's trivia at Hayweather House tonight," Luke said by way of greeting. Not even a "hello," or "hi," or "how are you on this fine Saturday?"

"We're all going to go, and you're coming too," he continued without waiting for a response.

"Oh." I tried not to sound startled. "Who is 'we'?"

"Adam, Daniel, Jack, Briseyda, Sarah. A bunch of the cohort. It starts at eight, so we'll be there to secure our table fifteen minutes early."

I didn't want to ask if Ivy would be there. I'd cried in bed last night thinking about the two of them together. It's not that I was jealous. I just kept thinking about how Ivy had everything—she was successful, popular, and she had a man who sounded like he was head over heels about her. She'd even had Luke, and the luxury of deciding she didn't want him. No, I wasn't jealous. I just felt bad for Luke.

I realized I'd been quiet for a little too long. "Okay." I breathed. "But I don't know how much help I'll be in bar trivia. See you then." Taking a page out of Luke's abrupt book of etiquette, I hung up without saying goodbye.

I actually thought I'd be pretty damn helpful at trivia. Grandma raised me watching *Jeopardy!* every night, and I loved being quizzed on random things. Again, probably an indicator of why I was in education.

I was flustered. Saturdays were usually a day that I didn't shower but lounged around in my sweats and greasy hair. I usually liked plenty of advanced notice before agreeing to any kind of social function.

Lucie knew that and consistently gave me shit about it. She was already gone for the night, having gone over to Amy's to get ready for wherever they were going. Since she'd turned twenty-one last year, Lucie went out every weekend, drinking and dancing and kissing—who knows what else—then came home to either have loud sex with Amy or to puke in our bathroom until 4 a.m., waking me up with every gag. She was the loudest vomiter I'd ever heard.

Already anxious for the unexpected social interaction, I lunged out of bed to get myself cleaned up.

***

Just a few hours later, I was on my way to Hayweather House. It was another on-campus bar (I know, how many could there be?) that was well-known for their array of beers on tap, their strong liquor mixes, and their game nights. I'd never been to one before.

The night wasn't too dark, as it was a big, clear full moon that night. The streets near campus were already flooded with the drunk and degenerate students, and I was happy to arrive at the inviting steps of my destination without much trouble.

Hayweather House was literally an old house, with once-beautiful hardwood floors now stained with years of sticky spills. Their wooden furniture sat on one side of the now open space, with billiards and a bar top on the other. It was fairly warm and inviting, but it was also loud.

I had never really enjoyed loud spaces, unless you counted classrooms. I had just walked in and was scanning the room when I saw Sarah waving me down at a nearby table. Sarah was in the cohort on the English teachers side—we still had a bunch of classes together, but I didn't talk to her much.

I kind of got the sense that she was just as quiet as I was, and maybe we were too similar to get anywhere with the friendship. She was also a younger, smaller-sized woman. She wore big glasses that made her look somewhere between a hipster and an academic. She didn't wear much makeup, and her clothes made her look like a librarian. But she was nice, and she waved me over to her table immediately.

Briseyda, a fiery thirty-something woman who went back to school to finish her degree, and Adam were already seated. No sign of Luke.

"Where is everyone else?" I asked, trying not to sound like I was pining.

It was Adam who answered. He was kind of a take-charge guy. He was seated across from Sarah and Briseyda, with vacant chairs on either side of him. The round tables were set up for teams of five or six members. I took a seat next to Sarah.

"Jack's on his way, he said to save him a seat, and—" He was cut off by a tall, broad-shouldered body leaning over the table, answering what he was going to say next. Luke was holding three drinks among all his fingers and knuckles, liquid slopping over the sides of each. He set down a beer in front of the chair next to me, the foam rolling down the glass onto the shiny wooden table.

"Who's ready to rock this trivia game? Winning is the only

option," he said without looking at any of us in particular. He silently handed Adam a clear liquor drink with a lime on the rim before he stepped around the backs of Briseyda's and Sarah's chairs. Briseyda and Sarah resumed their conversation, and I felt Luke pause behind my chair. He leaned behind me, his lips inches from my ear. Brushing my arm, he placed a tall drink in front of me. It was almost pink in color, save for the gray tone it took on from whatever was mixed in it.

"I knew you wouldn't want beer, but here's a real drink," he murmured in my ear, his breath tickling a few strands of my hair against my neck. Before I could reply, he was standing erect again, stepping around all the way to take his seat in between me and Adam.

I let him settle in his seat before I met his gaze and said, "Thank you," in an embarrassingly high but heavy voice.

He'd bought me a drink? Me, who hadn't even shown up yet when he went to the bar? He was anticipating my arrival then. And with two other women there, forced to go to the bar to get their own drinks . . .

I couldn't ignore the fact that he'd also bought Adam's drink as well. Maybe I was just his good friend, on the same level with Adam.

I took a sip from the straw in front of me and tried to school my face into an expression of someone who enjoyed an alcoholic beverage, not someone who drank so seldom that the taste of liquor never ceased to shock me. How could someone choose this drink over something actually satisfying?

"What is this?" I asked Luke, who was looking exceptionally sharp tonight. Actually, he looked the opposite of sharp. He looked relaxed.

In a career-readiness program like we were in, we basically always dressed like we were at job interviews. Student teaching is like an audition, and getting a good recommendation was paramount, so dressing the part was vital. We all dressed like the snazziest teachers you'd ever seen. It was a novelty to see someone like Luke in a fitted T-shirt and jeans. He looked damn good.

"It's Hayweather's Lemonade—their special. I thought you might like it. Lemonade with strawberry vodka and a bit of syrup to make it sweet." I didn't want to tell him it tasted like middle-schooler piss, so I just drank.

Everyone at our table small-talked about student teaching, overwhelm, and commissary until Jack showed up and took his seat by Adam before the trivia round began.

The trivia was trivial—some I knew, some I didn't. I wasn't a particularly competitive person, and I definitely wasn't in a competitive mood. I didn't speak up much unless I knew the right answer or had something valuable to contribute to the conversation.

Overall, I was kind of having fun. A superficial, drink-haze-induced kind of fun, and I knew I wouldn't still be sitting here if it weren't for Luke. He hadn't given me any specific attention, but to be included by him, to be given a drink by him, the most attractive guy in our cohort, felt significant to me. Maybe I was delusional, but I didn't care. Not when I felt this high. I had another lemonade, the second tasting better than the first, and the third tasting even better after that.

We had just finished the first trivia round when two things happened at once: A tipsy-from-two-gin-and-tonics Jack stood up, careening toward the bar for another, when he stumbled and almost took out a waitress. Not seeing him coming, the tray of glasses she carried tipped out of her hands, crashing to the floor in a spontaneous explosion of glass and sound. I hadn't seen it coming; I had been staring at Luke's smooth cheeks, wondering if his skin was that beautiful from a hygiene regimen or genetics. Having not seen the crash coming, I was caught unaware as a loud, explosive noise hit my ears, sending me into a place of panic I had never been in before.

I was frozen, like in a bad dream when you can't move, can't scream, as the bad guy is about to hurt you. My sense of hearing was incapacitated as my body went numb. Tingles up my body reached my eyes, making them water. Luke was looking at me then, and I wanted to move, I wanted to react, but my body was frozen.

It had been shots. Gun fire. Again, in front of me. Sammie was lying on the floor of the bar in front of me, half covered by a tarp. My heart was beating in my ears, my breaths coming quick.

I could see Luke's lips moving, but I couldn't understand what they were saying. Was he speaking to me? Was he looking at me? He moved in slow motion. My thoughts raced to the students; did they see anything? Did they need me? In a moment of discombobulation, I lost track of reality and where I was.

All at once, time came rushing back to full speed. The waitress was cleaning up broken glass; no one was bleeding. No one was dead.

The pounding in my ears subsided, but the tightness in my chest remained.

"You okay?" Luke asked me with genuine concern in his eyes as he took in my appearance.

I took a shallow breath and blinked back the wetness in my eyes. "Yeah," I said, trying to sound nonchalant. I didn't want to look like the baby getting scared by a loud noise. I didn't want to look like the freak who was scared of violence in our violent world. At this point, everyone near me had forgotten about the incident at my school the other week—they had no reason to know I would feel messed up.

What even was that? Why did I react that way and think about the incident *now?* I didn't give myself time to ponder it before I grabbed my third sweating glass of defiled lemonade, brought it to my lips, tipped my head back, and chugged.

I didn't remember much of the rest of that night.

Here was what I remembered: We lost trivia. Drunk Jack yelled about how we were robbed until we left, one by one trickling out into the night. At one point, Luke drew me into his chest, covering me from the rain in the front of his jacket. He said something that was hilarious, and I laughed until I could barely stand.

Somehow, I got home.

CHAPTER FIFTEEN

I WOULDN'T JUDGE LUCIE so harshly for her loud puking anymore. Not after what happened to me that next morning. I woke up still wearing my makeup from the night before, but at least I'd made it into some pajamas.

I awoke with a tight headache—not pounding, but sharp. And I definitely felt nauseous.

Breakfast, I thought. I just need some breakfast to absorb whatever is left in my gut.

I made my way into the kitchen and made myself a full meal: toast, scrambled eggs, diced potatoes that passed as hash browns. I couldn't remember the last time I'd made such a full meal, or had the time to, at least. I ate slowly, drinking water and taking two ibuprofen, hoping the headache would ease.

I was cleaning up my dishes when the second wave of nausea hit me like a train. I barely made it to the garbage can before I threw up. My hearty breakfast, my water, my drugs. All of it was wasted in the garbage. My stomach was in knots.

I got the shakes again, like I had the night of Lucie's birthday.

Uncontrollable, visceral shaking. I needed to warm up. And rest. Leaving the rest of the dishes for later, I dragged myself like a zombie back into my bedroom, where I turned up my heater. I crawled under my blankets, my head pounding now more than it had before. I barely moved an inch, for fear of nausea returning, until my shaking and writhing eased.

***

It was past two and I still hadn't heard from Lucie, so I called her. She answered on the second ring, and I could hear that she was somewhere decently loud.

"Hey, Rach, what's up?"

"I'm so sick. I've never been this hungover." It was all I could muster from my raw throat.

"Whoo! Go Rachel! Where'd you go last night?"

"I went to trivia with some cohort people. Am I that much of a lightweight?" I would have been embarrassed to admit it if I didn't feel so terrible. I already knew I wasn't going to tell Luke or the guys. Little miss twenty-one-year-old gets drunk off hard lemonade.

"Just try to sleep it off. You'll be fine," Lucie said.

"Do you think, on your way home, you could get me a Gatorade? I can't keep any water down. I've been puking every hour all day. I have nothing in my stomach, so it's just bile and acid. It tastes awful, and my throat hurts. My stomach hurts. Everything hurts."

I knew I was bordering on whiny, but I was scared. The ache in my head was so sharp from being so dehydrated, and I couldn't keep anything down. I was worried that soon I'd have to be that girl in the emergency room with alcohol poisoning who had to be on an IV drip.

Lucie didn't answer right away. "Um . . . yeah. Yeah, I can probably do that."

"Thanks, Luce. Will you be home soon?"

"In a little bit, yeah. Rest up. I'll be home later. Bye!" She hung up quickly.

I didn't really ask Lucie for much these days. I didn't pester her to clean up after herself. I didn't need her to give me rides anymore. I didn't mind asking her for a Gatorade, especially if she was already out. I hoped she didn't mind bringing me one.

And bring me *one* she did. One single, small Gatorade, at 7 p.m. By then, I'd showered, sitting down in the tub from weakness. I had given up on schoolwork and had been laying on my bed, staring at the ceiling, all afternoon. When Lucie came home with the Lemon Lime Gatorade in hand, I was grateful to have something to sip at, but I took it slow. I muttered my thanks, and she didn't hover for long.

I asked her if she thought I had some kind of predisposition to be intolerant to alcohol, and she said yeah, maybe. I felt better thinking that that was the problem, not that I couldn't handle the slightest bit of liquor.

The next day, I told Mrs. Means I had had food poisoning all weekend. It was better than admitting I had been out drinking like a senseless kid. She gave me some grace to sit down and observe in the back of the room during the lessons rather than being up and around helping with the students.

Mrs. Means had ceded her one class period to me—third period. She still required me to watch first and second periods, then granted me permission to emulate her lessons exactly in third period. The only way I could put my own spin on it was through my own questions during discussion time, if I could even get students to engage with me. They'd always been absolute nutcases, and keeping them quiet was a challenge anyway, but the last week since the "incident" had been hell.

It was like they had regressed years in their ability to pay attention, stay quiet, and stop hitting each other. Many students had been chronically absent and constantly needed reteaching. I'd be lucky to finish teaching about the Byzantine Empire by spring break.

Unfortunately, Monday was also the day I had to go observe Jared at Grant Middle School. I bid Mrs. Means adieu as I rushed out to my car to head across town to the fancy neighborhood. It was incredibly stark—you wouldn't believe Rocky Middle and Grant Middle existed in the same town.

Over by the Big Bend campus, on the north side of town, there was a small radius of run-down college housing before it opened into well-kept streets housing million-dollar dwellings. The yards were lush and immaculate, and no cars were parked on the street. Three-story homes towered above the streets. I had never lived in a neighborhood like this—and probably never would.

How could Mrs. Means live over here? Like, literally, how could she afford to live in one of these houses with a Rocky Middle salary? Her husband must have done something impressive.

It wasn't hard to find Grant Middle—not when it was a two-story rectangular building made entirely of glass. It looked brand new. I knew it was a few years old already, but it was the fanciest building I'd ever seen—let alone for a middle school. It definitely said something about the tax bracket of its neighborhood. Rocky was a one-story brick building that was older than anyone working there, and that was saying something.

I parked in visitor parking and headed for the big glass doors that appeared to be the main entrance. With everything transparent, it wasn't hard to locate the main office desk, get my visitor badge, and get instructions to Jared's classroom. It was on the second floor, the secretary pointed, my gaze following her hand as she gestured at the ceiling that, I'll be damned, was also made of glass that showed all the pipes running through. I left the office and headed up the glass stairs, trying not to look at my feet as I ascended to the second floor.

I was grateful my arrival had been timed during class—if it had been a passing period, I would have been overwhelmed by swarms of middle schoolers going to their next class.

I found Jared's classroom on the corner of the building. The glass walls bordering the hallway—opaque from large curtains—was a necessity, I'd imagine, with distractible middle schoolers. I only had to pace for a minute or two before the bell rang, and students spilled out of every classroom and into the halls. I backed against the glass wall facing outside, watching Jared's classroom door to ensure students had made their way out before I took a deep breath and stepped across the threshold. I was met by a bark.

"Not now!" Jared said, looking me dead in the eyes. He wasn't yelling, he wasn't whispering, but he was using a screaming tone in a speaking volume. Probably a skill that he utilized teaching middle schoolers.

Only then did I see the student facing him, clearly getting a talking to after class. I turned right around and retreated to the glass hallway, heat rising to my face. My neck felt sweaty, and my stomach was reeling.

I wasn't embarrassed that I'd walked in when I was unwanted. I felt like such a goddamn idiot for being in a position where someone could speak to me that way, and that I had simply taken it. What else could I do? He was in the position of power; he was helping me get my observation hours in when I didn't have other options.

I tried to calm myself as I felt students brushing past me down the hallway. I'd been staring at the glass beneath my feet when I straightened my spine. Fine, if he was going to be a jerk, then I would be as nice as possible, be accommodating, and not do anything else that could piss him off enough to speak in that tone to me again. The bell had already rung when he came out to get me.

"You can come in now," he said without looking at me. I followed him into his room, and I was at first surprised by how underwhelming it felt compared to the grandeur of the rest of the building. He had dark shades over the glass wall facing outside and no posters covering any surface. There was nothing personal about it at all.

He gestured over to a chair in the corner that clearly was my seat for the time being. As class had already started, Jared was scribbling a late pass for the student he was talking to before, and he instructed his students to begin logging in to their computers for a game.

There were only six students in the class. Not that I expected it to be the biggest class ever, given that it was advanced English learners in middle school, but only six students? If Rocky had ELD class, it would be packed with the children of migrant workers. But I had to keep in mind the demographics of the students in this area.

As Jared instructed them to log on to a website, I was bracing myself for them to get up and grab Chromebooks off the cart. I'd heard some of my cohort colleagues talk about how they had Chromebook carts in their classroom—a full class set of the Google mini laptops for student use. It sounded pretty fancy to me, especially since my alma mater high school had only one computer lab with massive desktop computers we could use.

No, Jared's six students weren't reaching for a Chromebook cart. They reached into their binders and each pulled out a shiny MacBook. They promptly opened them and set out to the game website. I must have looked extremely puzzled because Jared approached me then, if only to brag.

"Big Bend School District got one-to-one MacBooks this year," he stated simply.

"So each student has their own? That they can take home?" I asked in disbelief. He didn't say anything. He just nodded as he walked away to sit at his desk.

I watched as the thirteen-year-olds logged on to their individual computers that were newer and fancier than the one I had afforded myself before I began college. I'd never even heard of a school having Apple products.

Most of the schools I'd heard of with the cheap, small

Chromebooks were lucky to have classroom sets. At Rocky, there were two sets for the entire school to check out from the library. We had to reserve them in advance, and we were lucky if they had been plugged in to charge by the last class.

I'd known the kids in this neighborhood had more luxuries, but I didn't know they were *this* spoiled. Or privileged, should I say? I knew I should feel happy that these students were getting the best possible opportunities in public education, but again, I couldn't shake the feeling of dismay, thinking about the concept of deserving. Who really *deserved* the nicest things? And who should be the one deciding that?

I imagined this group of international students being spoon-fed from literal silver spoons, the finest caviar sliding into their baby mouths as their expensive nannies dabbed at their chins with a silk napkin.

It suddenly became very clear to me that this group of middle schoolers was so different from my group of middle schools because the demographics of this group were so different: These English learners weren't the children of migrant workers; these were the kids of the college professors who were brought in from countries abroad to teach their field of expertise.

These students weren't from the slums of Guatemala; they were from the suburbs of Hong Kong. Looking at the array of cultures present in the group of six students, I was gaining the feeling that I had stepped into another world. And some of my cohort colleagues were placed in schools like this? They were having a wildly different student-teaching experience than I was.

I looked back to Jared, who seemed immersed in something on his computer while his students played their online game independently.

It was the longest forty-five minutes of my life.

CHAPTER SIXTEEN

"HE KNEW I was coming into his class Monday to observe—for an assignment he gave us, no less—and yet he had his students playing a computer game all period! Can you believe that?" I asked Luke in between bites of pizza that Friday night.

Though we'd exchanged side glances all week during classes, we hadn't made much conversation until after Annabel's class.

He'd been on my mind all week. I imagined him piggybacking on me everywhere I went, his lips close to my ear, whispering when I was trying to focus on other things. The weight of him was with me everywhere I went, distracting me. Being in his presence now, one-on-one, when I had his full attention, I was elated. I was high. I felt lighter than I had all week. Or maybe for weeks now.

The most attention he'd given to me was at the beginning of Jared's class on Tuesday. He joked with me and Jack about some shot glass he'd stolen from Hayweather's House on Saturday night. I clearly had been unaware at the time, but at least I learned how I'd gotten home—the guys had walked me as far as the nearest cross street, at least.

I obviously made it the last half block alone and up into my apartment. I didn't know whether to feel grateful that they saw me most of the way home or a little peeved that no one made sure I was safe all the way there, but I couldn't be mad at anyone for not taking care of me. No one had ever really taken care of me.

Safe to say, by Friday night, I was starved for Luke's attention.

Logically, I knew I shouldn't like Luke. Realistically, I knew his history with women and alcohol were an unstable foundation for me to place any of my feelings in. He was a wild card, after all.

But under the soft, warm lighting of Rodeo's Pizza, he was everything I needed to take the edge off.

I'd never had an addictive personality. I'd never fallen for any of the typical addictive substances, unless you counted Pepsi. But looking at Luke's peach-pink lips while he talked on about himself, there was nowhere else I wanted to be.

He had listened to me talk for the first few minutes, which was rare. It didn't bother me that he seemed to dominate our conversations. He had interesting things to say, and his student-teaching placement was far more interesting than mine.

"She hates me!" he reemphasized to me. "I could do anything, and she'd be like 'Luke you need to work on this. Mr. Earnest, do I need to speak with your program manager about this?' She calls me out in front of the kids too. I can't wait to be in my own classroom and not have that hag breathing down my neck."

I smiled at the way he mocked her, putting on a high-pitched voice to match his sneer.

"I'm sorry she's so demanding of you. At least she has high standards! My cooperating teacher has no faith in me whatsoever."

"Why is that?" he asked. I couldn't tell if he was genuinely asking or if he was waiting to make a snippy remark.

I shrugged nonchalantly, like none of it bothered me. I didn't want to seem bothered.

"I guess she just hasn't seen how good I am yet." I smiled slightly, pleased with my own superficial confidence. I wanted Luke to believe I was confident. I was sure he went for confident girls. Like Ivy.

He finished his second slice of pizza and downed the last dregs of his beer. "Thanks again for the pizza," he hedged. "You didn't have to."

I kind of felt like I had to, though. Luke hadn't exactly been subtle when we stepped up to the counter earlier to order, and he paused and stepped out of the line to check his phone for a couple of minutes. Checking his bank account. Making sure he had enough money in his checking account to afford the two slices of pizza and one beer.

I felt awkward, trying not to look past his shoulder at his phone, but also not wanting to hold up the line. So I just bought our slices and drinks and said it was my treat.

Even though he had suggested this date, or hangout, or whatever this was, I didn't have to worry about buying a couple slices of pizza. I knew I had enough money in my bank.

Luke had never been quiet about student loans before, so it made sense. I just wasn't expecting him to turn it back around on me.

The air hung with the silence of his gratitude. We were both clearly thinking about money.

"When we graduate, are you going to look for a job with loan forgiveness?" he asked.

Some school districts in rural or run-down areas had state-funded programs of loan forgiveness. It was kind of an unspoken thing that some of us pretty much had no choice but to seek jobs in Title I schools.

"I hadn't really thought about it too much. I'm just hoping to get a job at all," I said honestly.

"Oh, we'll get jobs," he said so assuredly. "We'll scour every job fair in the state in the spring." I liked the way he said *we*. "But how do you plan to get out of the loan debt if you don't work in a Title I school?"

I wasn't usually comfortable talking about finances with people, because I didn't want to sound too privileged, but I told Luke the truth.

"I'm not in any debt. Besides my car payments, anyway. I get monthly insurance payments that have helped me stay afloat. Not that they'll last forever, but yeah. I'm okay."

He didn't let it go—no, not Luke. When he was curious about something, he pushed. "Insurance for what?"

I sighed. Might as well be fully open. My eyes downcast on the table, I told him about my family.

"When my mom died in a car accident about twelve years ago, she had a decent life insurance policy set up. The beneficiaries were listed as both me and my dad, but he didn't want any part of it. He started drinking heavily, and he ended up just kind of . . . walking away. That's how I ended up living with my grandma. When I turned eighteen, the insurance payments started coming directly to me in monthly installments."

I peeked up at him. He didn't say anything for a moment, but he was looking at me with softened eyes.

"I've still had to work throughout school to supplement it," I went on. "And the money runs out this summer, but it's how I've gotten through college. I never could have done it otherwise."

All he said was "Give me your hand."

There, in the loud pizza parlor, he held my hand softly on top of the table, grazing his thumb back and forth across my knuckles.

CHAPTER SEVENTEEN

IT NEVER SNOWED in Big Bend. The winters were extremely wet, yes, but it was at such a low elevation that when the forecast called for snow, I brushed it off. No, it never snowed here. Not even a light dusting. Just torrential rain all winter.

That's what I kept telling myself, anyway, Sunday night as heavy clouds loomed over my apartment building. There was absolutely no chance. Maybe I'd just always been a pessimist.

I hadn't even gotten out of bed the next morning when I got a call from Mrs. Means.

Snow day.

I crawled out of my bed long enough to peek through the curtains of my bedroom. Sure enough, a few inches of snow covered everything. Snow in Big Bend! Back home in the mountainous part of the state, it took at least a foot of snow for them to call for the day off. Here, all it took was a couple inches, apparently. But I wasn't complaining as I climbed back in between my flannel sheets and dozed until nine.

By the time I got up, there were at least six inches of snow, with huge chunks of flaky snow still falling from the sky. Lucie was up too, dressing to go out. It wasn't her usual "going out" attire—this morning she was clad in her tallest rain boots, a knit hat with a pom-pom on top, and her rain jacket over a hoodie and another sweater. People didn't usually come to Big Bend equipped to make snow angels, so I was impressed with her innovative layers.

She gave me a look like she was surprised to see me. Did she think I'd be at school on a day like this, or was she not expecting to talk to me this morning?

"Going sledding?" I mused, knowing full well there were no hills in the vicinity.

She raised her eyebrows and scoffed. "We're all heading to campus to walk around. Amy and August are already on the quad. They said the streets are totally shut down! Like, the city has no snowplows, and so everyone's just out in the streets."

I waited a moment, wondering if she might invite me along. When she didn't say anything, but instead reached for her purse, I told her, "Well, have fun. Be safe. I'll probably be around here most of the day."

She muttered thanks and goodbye and left. It felt so quiet, standing in our kitchen alone in the midmorning. A rarity for me. A great day to get ahead on schoolwork, I guess.

I made a festive cup of hot chocolate before heading back up to my room to settle in on my bed/workspace/dining room. I had stared at my computer for about two hours when I threw in the towel, laid back against my pillows, and flipped on the TV. I looked through a few different apps, debating a few shows, but settled back on *Sex and the City*. I had seen every episode a dozen times, but it was comforting to have a familiar show on.

The snow continued to fall. When I was tired of listening to Carrie Bradshaw deal with unavailable men, I started puttering around: picking up my closet, wiping down the bathroom counter, cleaning out the fridge.

When I got too antsy, I ventured out of the apartment, down the alleyway to the mailbox, which, of course, was empty. No one was delivering today. Lucie was right—the roads were absolutely shut down. Despite being afternoon, the roads were still covered in eight or nine inches of snow. No snowplows in sight. No one shoveling snow off their steps or sidewalks. Big Bend really didn't have the resources for this. They were utterly unprepared. It was eerie.

College students filled the streets. It was like one big snow-themed sorority bash. They had to have been drinking heavily—otherwise, they'd all be freezing in their light rain jackets and jeans. They mostly looked soaked to the bone, like they'd been playing in the snow like kids.

It would have been endearing if it wasn't so goddamn annoying.

Music was blasting throughout the neighborhood. I could feel it, the low bass reverberating through my boots. Laughing and screaming ricocheted off the close buildings as they threw snowballs and made snow angels.

Many of these students had probably never seen such high amounts of fluffy snow on the ground. I wanted to feel excited for them, but all I felt was disgruntled at the fact that they were having fun while I was trying to get work done. It was oddly similar to how I felt the day I got the massage from Cole—how could I wish "growing up" upon those who were so clearly young at heart? Was I just mad that they had something I didn't? The resentment didn't feel good.

I went back inside, sliding off my soaked shoes by the heater, and retreated back to my bedroom, where I cranked up the heat and got underneath the blanket. I had the shakes again. Shivering violently, I pulled out my phone to scroll through social media.

As I looked at the photos already posted by Lucie, Amy, August, and a handful of other college students I followed, my shaking seemed to get worse. Maybe my hands were too cold. I put my phone down and pulled my hands under the blanket, shivering until

I fell asleep for the majority of the afternoon.

When it hadn't stopped snowing by nightfall, they called a second snow day early.

And another one after that.

And when the snow still hadn't cleared by Wednesday night, they called it for the rest of the week. I'd never heard of a school district taking an entire week off for snow—and I might have been as ecstatic as everyone else, if I wasn't so goddamn lonely.

I sat at home on my own all week. I hadn't heard from anyone, and I hadn't ventured out either. The snow kept the town shut down: the roads were still unplowed, the mail still hadn't been delivered, and the college students were still going feral. I ate what was in the fridge and watched old shows.

I wanted to know what Luke was doing, who he was with, if he was one of the drunk people partying in the streets or if he'd taken a responsible approach like me and tried to get ahead on school projects and lesson plans.

But I didn't call him. I looked at my phone, willing him to call me, but he never did.

Lucie was gone all week, coming home only briefly for dry socks, but I kept up with her escapades via her social media feeds. It looked like they'd all been having a ball.

It was kind of self-pitying, I knew, to stay inside and wish I was having fun when I wasn't reaching out to anyone else either, but I wanted to feel chosen. I wanted them to *want* to include me. I wanted to know that people wanted me to be around, not that I was forcing them to be close with me. So I didn't call, and I didn't reach out.

It was Saturday night by the time I started running low on food. I'd gotten creative and used some cheese and the last few drops of milk to make a kind of macaroni and cheese on the stove top. I was sitting down to eat it in front of my TV when my phone vibrated demandingly.

It was Luke. Finally, it was Luke. My heart began to race, and I didn't take the chance to be couth before I answered it immediately.

"Hey," I said, almost breathlessly.

"Damn it's nice to hear your voice." His voice was low, gravelly. "How are you surviving the snow-pocalpse?" he asked cheerfully. He had this charming way of being silly yet sultry at the same time.

I didn't want to let my bitterness and self-pity show. If his imagination ran as wild as mine did, I didn't want him to envision me curled up in my bed, not having washed my hair in four days, like I currently looked. Greasy and sad.

"Well, it's really freaking cold. I've pretty much been wrapped up in my blankets all week. What have you been up to?"

"Mmm, sexy," he replied, his voice low. Had he been drinking? Maybe he *had* been one of those rowdy drunks outside . . .

"If we ever get out of this igloo, are we on for pizza after Annabel's class next week? I've missed you." My heart fluttered at the thought of him missing me this week.

I wanted to say that that was almost a whole week away, and I didn't want to wait that long to see him, but I wanted to play it cool. So I just said, "Hell yeah. Your beer is on me."

CHAPTER EIGHTEEN

FOR ONCE, MRS. Means had the courtesy of calling me the night before she threw me in the deep end.

On Sunday evening she called to inform me that her husband was in the hospital—he'd fallen during their ski trip. He had badly broken his leg and needed surgery, and she'd be out for at least three days, maybe more, as she took care of him.

She wanted me to come in anyway—in fact, she wanted me to run the classroom this week. She asked if I could stay all day and teach all of her history classes. Of course, I'd be under the supervision of a substitute teacher, but I'd be in charge.

I didn't want to think about how condescending it was that even though I was taking all of these education-based classes and working toward being a certified teacher, not to mention that these students knew me, an adult that didn't know the school and probably didn't have anything but a substitute license would be watching over me.

Still, the pressure was on. Impressing Mrs. Means by not letting her classes fall apart for the better of a week? Let alone when students were coming off a week of unexpected days off? Sure to be chaos. But I knew this was definitely my chance to prove myself.

Especially when Mrs. Means once again brought up the benefit of my résumé at the end of our phone call.

"Seriously, thank you so much, Rachel." I didn't think she'd ever use my given name. "If you can pull this off, I'll write you the most amazing recommendation letter."

"It's really no problem. I'd be there anyway, I know the curriculum, and I know the ki—students. I'll handle it."

I didn't have to reassure her much more before she hung up. I don't think she really cared that much about leaving her classroom in someone else's care, but more about ensuring she was covered to spend time at home with her husband. I couldn't really blame her.

The next morning, I trudged across town through the snow. Luckily, I had purchased a car that could make the trek over the mountain pass that took me to my hometown while Grandma was still there, so I knew I'd be okay in the snow. However, other people were not.

Half the battle in driving in winter conditions is defensive driving. People got nervous, slammed on their brakes, and slid back and forth. The key was to relax, take it easy, and slow down.

That was probably the key to life, but I wasn't good at following my own advice.

I eased across town on roads that still hadn't been plowed but had been packed down by days of people driving on them. I didn't have to slam on my brakes once.

Still, I felt relieved to pull into the parking lot at Rocky Middle, which was an odd feeling, I'll admit. I never felt happy pulling into Rocky.

I was right about the students being absolutely wild. Something about long weekends or breaks in school made students go feral. They wanted to talk, they wanted to play, and today, they wanted to throw snowballs. The school had to announce before first period even began that throwing snow was absolutely off-limits, even though most of the kids were already soaked to the bone.

Here was one benefit of being the friendly, well-known student teacher when the real teacher is gone: The supervising substitute becomes the common enemy. Sure enough, the eighty-one-year-old Mrs. Walker had become the bad cop to my good cop, even if she didn't have much policing to do. Just the threat of her presence made the students align themselves with me, and despite being cold and a week behind on the Byzantine Empire, we were cruising.

Of course, between every class, Mrs. Walker had to toddle up to me to give me some remark about how I *should* teach, as she had taught elementary school before she retired twenty years ago. She was swell.

I imagined her like a vulture, in the rafters above me, as I performed an opera in a performance hall, heckling me with her cackles as I tried my best to sing my heart out for an already unforgiving audience.

I knew I shouldn't be so harsh to Mrs. Walker, even in my own head. She was just trying to give me some advice. And it made me feel good that, for the first time, students seemed genuinely happy that I was there, excited that I was leading them instead of the decrepit old lady.

The week went off without much of a hitch. As I expected, Mrs. Means was out for four days, and when she came back on Friday, she was so discombobulated that I ended up teaching anyway.

The students were still on their best behavior, enjoying the reprieve of my teaching over Mrs. Means's, but I knew it was only because it was a novelty. It was a classic honeymoon period, and it was sure to come to an end at some point.

I was grateful, though, that the students had worked in my favor to help me impress Mrs. Means. I would have literally thanked them, if I didn't think it would wreck some of my credibility as a responsible adult. I didn't want them to think they had enough power to take down my career, though that's certainly how it felt at times.

Mrs. Means had no problem with me teaching her classes after that.

CHAPTER NINETEEN

THE NEXT WEEK, things hit a new low. The school district's attorney, Amanda Jones, was back, and she wanted to speak with all of us. We had to gather after school to hear the statement.

I went to the library with the rest of the teachers to hear the official business. As we filed in, I wasn't surprised to see Jones, the principal and vice principal, and half a dozen police officers at the front of the room.

I couldn't help but hope that when my student teaching was over, I wouldn't have to see so many police in school again.

I followed Mrs. Means to a table in the middle of the front of the room, though I would have much preferred to be by the windows or closer to the door. The cops still made me nervous. I didn't like that I could see their guns on their hips.

The visual of the weapons just made my mind race—it reminded me that they could be used with lethal force in seconds. I didn't think anyone needed to have that kind of killing power attached to them at all times. I had always felt that way, and I wasn't sure whether my opinion had changed after all of this.

If Sammie hadn't been armed, then Officer Ron wouldn't have shot them. If no lethal weapons had been present and available, then maybe Sammie's son would have both parents. And Ron wouldn't be on leave. And our students wouldn't be so terrified. And I wouldn't feel so on edge all the time.

I could torture myself forever wondering exactly what happened. I was the kind of person who needed to know the details of what happened to understand. I feared I'd never get closure.

I'd let my mind race while other people had been chitchatting before the start of the meeting, and my palms were sweaty. I willed myself to look anywhere but the holstered pistols. Mrs. Cairns, the principal, began the meeting.

"Hey, everyone, thanks for sticking around after school for this. It's important that we touch base as a staff with the investigation. We wanted to make sure you had a heads-up before the story breaks in the news this evening. The investigation is over."

The room was silent as we waited with bated breath. What was the verdict?

Cairns went on, "Officer Ron has been found not guilty, and the death of Sammie Lopez has been declared self-defense."

Still, no one spoke. "Ron will remain on leave until he is ready to come back to work. He is still shaken up."

I peeked at Mrs. Means as her eyebrows rose. I was relieved to see she was as surprised as I was. I couldn't believe the verdict had been reached so quickly. With the state attorney general involved, I figured it would take months. Government processes have a way of dragging out. I was also amazed that Ron was in the clear. With the current state of politics, I knew this would cause a riot. I knew immediately that that was why they called this meeting—to prep us for what was to come.

This wasn't over yet.

"Additionally"—it was now the attorney who spoke—"with the

release of the verdict tonight, the body camera footage from Officer Ron will be released to the public. This was something we tried to fight, but the AG didn't budge. They are using it to demonstrate the authenticity of Ron's innocence. They think it will help his case with the public, so it will be published this evening as well."

Murmurs began throughout the room. It was Mr. Tyler, the English teacher whose room I stepped into on that day, who spoke above all else. He didn't bother with the formality of raising his hand to speak; he simply demanded answers.

"What does this mean for us?" he asked loudly. The police exchanged glances. I wondered what they were thinking, how they felt about all of this. Probably relieved it had been Ron and not them. I thought about the little kids who thought they wanted to grow up to be cops. Little kids never thought they would one day have to deal with things like this. Or deal with them right now, in school. Were they proud to be cops?

"The thing is," Mrs. Cairns began after looking to the attorney for permission to speak, "cases like this have a way of becoming incredibly controversial. A police-involved death of a person of color would already spark interest, let alone that this person was a member of the LGBT community, and the fact that this all happened at a public school in West Big Bend. We want you to be prepared once more to expect . . . feedback . . . from the community."

"More protests," Mr. Tyler said matter-of-factly. Not asking a question. Stating what was to come. Nothing too big had hit the school yet, as far as community impact went, but there was a lot of talk online about how the district was handling the situation.

"Most likely, yes," answered the attorney. "It would help our school community heal if you don't make a spectacle of yourself, don't engage with any of it, online or otherwise, and just keep doing what you do best: teaching."

Damn, she was good. So rehearsed. She should have been in public relations instead of law. But I guess that's kind of what she was doing anyway, working for the school district.

We were dismissed. I walked quickly to my car, not wanting to linger any longer than I had to. I wanted to get home. Probably to an empty house. Lucie hadn't wanted to hang out much lately. It almost felt like she was cutting me off, the way she would practically dart out of a room when I entered. We hadn't held a conversation past a few sentences in weeks, and she was out of the house most of the time anyway.

Before I got in my car, I scanned the parking lot. Come tomorrow, there might be news reporters or angry community members picketing here. I was so tired of this.

No one in my program had mentioned the incident since that Friday in Annabel's class. Was it possible that they had forgotten? I wasn't sure, but I certainly didn't want this latest news to renew anyone's interest in me for it. I didn't want my classmates or professors to take notice of me because of this. I didn't want that attention.

But I couldn't let myself think too much about what would happen to me tomorrow—I had enough to worry about with the body camera footage coming out tonight. It was all that occupied my thoughts as I drove home.

Should I watch it? *Would* I watch it?

Would it make me feel better or infinitely worse about the whole thing? Would it actually show someone dying? I'm sure they couldn't get that graphic—Sammie's family would never have allowed that, given the choice. But I guess as they were considered a perpetrator in this situation, maybe they didn't get the right to privacy.

What a shitty, shitty situation. I hated that I was even near it.

I was right, and Lucie was nowhere to be seen when I got home. I didn't have class, so I turned on some TV reruns and laid on my bed for a while. I couldn't be bothered to make any dinner, and I didn't feel like eating anyway. I was too nervous for the news release.

The Daily Jade broke the news first: "State Attn. General Rules Fatal Shooting of Armed Suspect at Rocky Middle School Justified."

I skimmed the article, looking for any information I didn't already have. The article included an aerial shot from the day of Sammie's death, the tarp covering their body clearly in view, as well as my car right out front, surrounded by police tape and blocked from the street by an emergency response truck.

The story wrote everyone's names in full—Sammie's son and his mom, Officer Ron, the police chief who reported to the scene. I guess we were past protecting people's identities.

In the middle of the story was the part I was dreading: the body camera footage.

I paused. I told myself I wasn't stalling, but I knew I was hesitating, if only for a moment. I knew watching this would make me feel different—I just wasn't yet sure if it would be for the better or worse.

I clicked play on the video.

It was exactly like I imagined. The footage began during passing period, with dozens of my familiar students walking by in the background as Officer Ron addressed Sammie in the hallway outside the main office. No one was arguing violently yet; they were just having a discussion that was rising in tension every second.

Ron told Sammie they needed to leave, or he was going to have to escort them out. Mrs. Cairns was there too, off camera. Her voice could be heard behind Ron, explaining that they could not relinquish a student to a noncustodial parent without prior clearance.

At that moment, the woman who had to be Shane's mother came through the doors, already raising her voice. She was storming toward the officer and Sammie, yelling something unclear through the body-cam microphone about how inappropriate this was and that they needed to leave.

Officer Ron said they both needed to calm down or leave the building due to the dispute rising in aggression, and the school wasn't the place for it. He demanded that Sammie leave. The mother was told to go to the office to check the paperwork for accuracy concerning Shane.

Sammie grew more agitated. They were yelling that they refused to leave without their child, even as Ron reached to guide them out. When Sammie still refused, getting more aggressive and defiant, Ron grabbed Sammie's arms to escort them from the building.

They were just through the doors when Sammie began flailing, doing all they could to escape the hold of Ron, then twisted with their right hand to reach in their jacket pocket, pulling out a small handgun. A 9 mm pistol, the article had said.

Sammie barely had it out of their jacket before they pulled the trigger, the aim clearly unfocused; the bullet hit nothing. Not a second passed before Ron had his own gun unholstered and aimed at Sammie's head.

The footage showed Ron's hand aimed at Sammie, but the fatal blow was cut off the screen. I was grateful for it. The footage stopped with Ron standing up, above Sammie's body.

Frozen for a moment after the footage stopped, I blinked away the images and continued reading the article. Somehow, it got worse.

After the search and investigation, Sammie was revealed to have had extra rounds for the handgun in their other jacket pockets and additional magazines in their car. They had come to the school, or perhaps went prepared everywhere they went, to fight somebody. Begin a fight or end a fight.

So it was ruled as self-defense and the defense of others. Was it in defense of the students and people in the school building or in defense of other cops?

And maybe it truly was. All Ron knew was that this person, who he'd perceived as a threat, pointed a gun at him.

I felt sick to my stomach. I had thought that it was clear who was in the wrong—that any police killing of a person of color, armed or not, was part of a systemic issue.

But when that person pulls the gun on you first? Pulls the gun and *fires*? There's simply not enough time to consider where you stand on it, I guess, before you're pulling the trigger.

My mind numb, my hand reached for my phone. Without thinking about it, I was dialing Luke. It rang twice before he answered.

"Was just thinking about you," he drawled in his charming way.

"Hey, are you home? Do you want to do something tonight?" I was eager for some human attention. From someone other than twelve-year-olds. I could have sat there alone with my thoughts, but I was sick of my thoughts. My stupidly visual brain couldn't stop seeing the guns pulled out, aimed directly at each other. I couldn't stop feeling like I was Officer Ron, and this was my perspective. I really wished I hadn't watched that damn video.

But I knew myself, and I was always going to watch it. There was no scenario, no version of myself, where I would have gone without knowing what happened, even if the images were burned in my mind forever.

I was relieved when Luke simply said, in a haughty voice, "Come over."

I was out the door in minutes. I grabbed my shoes and jacket, not bothering to grab my school stuff. Despite not really needing it, I always took my computer, under the guise that I intended to work with him on something. Because we were school friends.

But I didn't grab it this time. He sent me his address, and I walked the blocks to his house while the sun was going down, hustling down the sidewalk so fast that someone might have thought I stole something. He was opening the door mere seconds after my first knock.

He led me through the door before he promptly shut it behind himself. As soon as he turned to face me, he was wrapping me in a hug. A deep, warm hug. My eyes nearly brimmed with tears. This was what I needed. The house was quiet—I didn't see or hear a single roommate milling about. For such a college-boy house, it was fairly quiet.

Silently, he walked me to his bedroom. He wasn't his usually talkative self; he was softer somehow. He wasn't dominating the silence with his own voice; he was simply letting it be. Did he sense that I needed some peace? Or was this just him without a mask on—the raw, undiluted Luke, when he wasn't being someone else for the world to see?

I casually sat on the edge of his bed without saying anything. His bed was soft, the mattress broken in the way I preferred mine, though I tried not to let my mind wander to who had worn his in.

Did Ivy ever come here, or were they only at her place?

I didn't want to think about Ivy right now.

Any negative thoughts were prone to spiral. I was already too much in my head, as our silence had gone on for too long. I took my shoes off and brought my feet underneath me. His quilt had seen better days, but I liked that it felt homey and genuine. It wasn't trying to be a polished, perfect bedroom, the way Luke always seemed to be trying to come across as polished and perfect.

I looked around his room, at the type of decor he displayed. No photos of family or friends, but enough knickknacks and books that it was clear he made an effort with his space to reflect his tastes and interests. He was looking at me, waiting for me to say anything, his eyebrows slightly raised.

"Rough day," I said. I didn't want to explain. Maybe he already knew, anyway. Maybe he'd seen the news release and knew it would upset me. But I didn't want to bring it up if he hadn't.

"Mmm." He pressed his lips together and seemed to consider. "So you're not here to get ahead on the project for Jared's class?" He had a slight smirk as he said it, but he sat next to me on the bed.

I shook my head slowly. "No, I just needed to get out."

"So what do you want to do? I was going to make dinner. Want some?"

No one had ever made me dinner. Lucie was a miserable cook, and Grandma had practically raised me on canned soup and TV dinners.

I nodded. "What were you going to make?"

He made salads. I was surprised that such a strapping guy made salads for dinner, but I was impressed with his healthy choice. Most people in our program had either gained or lost weight throughout this year already, and Luke seemed in good shape still.

I was thinner than I'd ever been in my adult life. Eating hadn't been my priority the last few months. My granola bar for breakfast, the free snack during second period, and my one meal a day between student teaching and classes weren't really cutting it for maintaining a healthy weight. I wasn't hungry most of the time, though. Stress will do that to you.

I was wasting away. *Would anyone notice, though?* If my grandma was here, would she tell me to eat something? Or would she congratulate me on my unintentional crash diet? She was old like that—if anyone had lost weight, intentionally or not, it was cause for celebration, not concern.

I sat at the kitchen table (a college-boy house with a real kitchen table? Unheard of!) while Luke prepared the salads. He was so comfortable in his own space, so relaxed. It was sexy. Luke was already an incredibly attractive man, but watching him here, in his element, in his T-shirt and basketball shorts, I was more attracted to him than ever. I wanted to be closer to him.

We talked about our classes, people in the program, and music he was into; then he brought my salad bowl over to me—iceberg lettuce, chicken, cherry tomatoes, cilantro. Smothered in Italian dressing. I picked around the tomatoes without saying anything.

Luke wasn't always the most observant, but when he noticed something, he spoke up.

"You don't like tomatoes?"

"I mean, I like them in stuff, but eating them whole like this is a little too sweet for me." I tried to be apologetic. Instead of saying anything, he reached his fork into my bowl and began plucking the tomatoes out one by one, eating them as he went.

It made me smile. I felt like I hadn't smiled in days, like my face could finally contort that way.

The salad, sans tomatoes, was delicious. I'd never thought to put cilantro in a salad like that, and I was in love with it. Or maybe it was just because Luke had made it.

We finished eating in relative silence, and then I offered to help clean up, even though not much damage had been done in the kitchen.

I grabbed our bowls and brought them to the sink. I knew he had gotten up, but I was caught off guard when his hands lightly grabbed ahold of my waist from behind. My heart fluttered, as just his touch on my waist made me the best kind of nervous. Besides our comforting hand-holding in public, he hadn't touched me very much. We hadn't crossed that boundary.

His hands spun me around slowly to face him. His face was very close, as he was leaning down to me. He smelled divine, his warmth mixed with a masculine musk. It wasn't strong enough to make me think it was cologne—it was just him.

I felt his eyes on my lips as his hands slid all the way around my waist, embracing me closely. "Rachel." He breathed into my face.

It was almost my undoing. I still had my wits about me enough to ask in a whisper, "Won't this change everything? I don't want to ruin our friendship."

He responded only by moving his hands to either side of my face and leaning in closer. We were a centimeter from touching our lips. He paused, and I knew he was waiting for me to initiate the rest of the way to him.

For a few precious seconds, my mind raced, battling with itself. I imagined it split in two, the two sides of me arguing with each other. One side said, *Wait, where could this go? You shouldn't ruin a friendship just because of your desires*, while the other side screamed, *I WANT THIS MAN. LET ME HAVE HIM!*

I let the louder voice win.

I took in the scent of him one more time before I leaned the rest of the way and gently brushed my lips against his. Just once, before backing up slightly.

His responding groan of contentment was the best noise I'd ever heard. It made my heart ache in my chest, and parts of me ache lower too.

He came back immediately for another kiss. And another. His perfect amount of facial hair tickled my upper lip as my lips parted for him, and his tongue gently roved through my mouth. It was better than I could have imagined it, except one thing: He tasted like tomatoes.

CHAPTER TWENTY

I STAYED AT LUKE'S until past midnight. We kissed, talked, and kissed some more, until we found ourselves back on his worn-in quilt.

We were back to kissing, tongues intertwining, when he reached under my shirt and pulled it up. I raised my hands to his to pull my shirt back down. I was really into the kissing, but I wasn't ready to give him everything just yet.

I wanted Luke, I really did. At least, my body did. But my mind still knew that Luke easily grew tired of his playthings, and I didn't want to be cast aside if he grew bored of me too quickly. In spite of myself, I'd have to play his games to keep this up. If I wanted to keep him around me. And I needed him around me right now.

So he walked me home. He threw a hoodie on, hood up, and took a minute to calm down his excitement that I could clearly see through his basketball shorts, try as he might to hide it.

He walked with me in the dark until we reached my alleyway apartment, where he gave me a long kiss goodnight. I usually didn't like public displays of affection, but kissing in the middle of the night, lit only by a streetlamp, was so romantic, it was nearly knee-weakening.

I wanted the moment to last forever because I knew I had worse moments to face in the morning.

Despite staying up so late, my morning wasn't a chore; it wasn't a drag. I was still running on the high of last night and the streetlamp kiss.

I was still in a good mood, but I was apprehensive. Considering the outrage sparked following the incident at Rocky Middle, I could only imagine people's reactions after seeing it unfold on camera.

I was right to be worried. As I pulled up to the Rocky parking lot, I had to slow my car down to a crawl. Though it was only 8 a.m., two dozen people already stood outside the school with signs. They were shouting at cars as they pulled up. Shouting at children trying to get to school? Shouting at their parents?

I was no exception. They looked at me through my windshield as I drove through the lot, yelling what sounded like chants of "Justice for Sammie!" and "All Cops Are Bastards!"

I wasn't scared, but I was upset that they were using that language in front of my students. I was ready to run into the school as soon as my car door was shut and locked, but when I turned around, I noticed there wasn't the usual crowd of students waiting to be let in.

That was a first.

As I approached the doors, I could see dozens of students in the hallways inside. The door was still locked, but I didn't even have to knock before one of my seventh graders let me in. I went straight to Mrs. Means's room. Her door was closed too, but she let me in fairly quickly, closing the door and shutting all of the students outside it promptly.

"Cairns emailed this morning. We're going to start letting students inside the doors in the morning, at least until the attention outside dies down."

I hated her choice of words.

It continued like that for days. The protesters outside gathered in the morning, but they were usually burned out by noon. By the third day, a counter protest appeared, with parents picketing in favor of the protection of their children from harm.

It was complicated and confusing. For me, for local authorities, and most definitely for the students. I was impressed by their ability to keep their heads down and come to class, but anyone would have noticed that they had changed. Some of them were still acting like young and afraid children, like pee-pants Charles, but most of them were more mature than I'd ever seen them be.

I tried to add excitement to the class. I tried to add joy. I taught with such overdone enthusiasm that I thought I'd rupture a blood vessel in my head.

They were quiet. Not even a respectful quiet, like a reserved, "please don't look at me or talk to me" kind of quiet. Like their spirits were broken. They couldn't go outside for after-lunch recess break anymore, and the tension around the school was palpable.

These students used to drive me crazy. I used to think they'd be the end of my teaching career, driving me past my point of no return, but now I just felt horrible for them. I'd do anything to take away their hurt. I'd do anything to take this away.

I found my newest source of anxiety: feeling powerless.

CHAPTER TWENTY-ONE

MRS. MEANS AND I didn't talk about much outside of school, but I think that was more because I'm not a very loquacious person and I keep things to myself, and she was too selfish to ask. So it surprised me when she invited me to dinner.

"I'd love it if you could come by one night this week, I'll cook, and you can meet my husband. We can talk about your future and where you're headed next."

I liked that she was considering my next steps; it made me feel more like she trusted me to be successful now. My delayed response must have shaken her, because she went on, "It'll be my thank-you for taking over while Rick was down for his surgery. And I know he'd like to say his thanks too. Which night are you free?"

She wasn't really giving me much of a choice, but in all honesty that was the way to get me to engage in an activity I wasn't keen on. I needed to be backed into a corner before I'd say yes. So I said yes. After all, I was still trying to get on her good side.

It was Thursday already, so my days off were limited. With spring break in just a couple of weeks, my weekend would be spent making up any and all work I'd be slacking on. This program didn't have a lot of tests, but damn did it have a bunch of giant projects and papers.

"I'm free tonight," I said, "but I have class tomorrow. I know, Friday night classes are lame."

"Tonight, then!" she said, the most excited I'd ever seen her. "Come over around six? I'll text you my address."

I was dreading it, but I smiled anyway. At least meals had a set end point in which you could leave, unlike other social situations. Besides, I was a tiny bit curious about where she lived.

I didn't rest at all when I got home. I was too nervous. I hated dinner-party type situations anyway, but going to Mrs. Means house and meeting her family somehow intimidated me even more. I didn't know whether I should change, dress up, or if that would look like I was trying too hard since she already saw me at school in what I was wearing. I stared at my closet doors for most of the afternoon.

In the end, I decided to keep on what I was wearing, but I'd throw my hair in a chic bun. Very adult.

Never one to be late, I locked my door behind me and got into my car at 5:45, even though I knew it would only take me a few minutes to reach her house. As soon as she texted me her address, I put it in my app on my phone to assess the location. I memorized the street name and house number, then worked to memorize each and every turn I'd have to make so that I wouldn't have to look at my phone.

Her house was up on the hillside, like I suspected, where a lot of the nicer houses sat above the campus. Hers wasn't the nicest on the street, but it was an extremely nice street—the kind where you couldn't show your garbage cans, and the sidewalks were kept completely free of debris. I'd never live in a neighborhood like this, but it looked like a safe place.

Then again, schools should be a safe place too.

I parked along the curb, though there were no other cars on the street. I assumed it was fine enough guest parking.

I had shown up empty-handed. After all, *she'd* invited *me*. I thought about stopping by the store to get some wine, but I decided against it. I didn't even know which type of wine would be good, and I was sure Mrs. Means would know better. I didn't want to look foolish.

So, I ascended the steps to her front door with nothing in my hands. I rang the doorbell, which appeared to have a camera and an intercom system. Luckily, I didn't need to use either, because the door swung open to reveal a short, fat, bald man.

His shirt was buttoned down far enough to see his chest hair and a gold chain. His dark eyes and goatee made him look like a movie character who would be in an underground mob business. My mind pictured him sitting in a wingback chair, forcing people to bow down and kiss his ring.

He smiled. "You must be Rachel," he said like he knew me already. He was definitely the welcoming type. "I'm Rick, Isa's husband. Come in! Can I take your jacket?"

I smiled as I walked through the door, moving to take off my jacket, but his hands were already reaching to pull it from my shoulders. I guess they were really formal here, taking guest's jackets for them. I wasn't a super touchy person, though, so I tensed up. It only lasted a second before he was guiding me, hand an inch away from touching the small of my back, toward their dining room.

It smelled good. I took in my surroundings. Mrs. Means certainly had interesting tastes at home—apart from the Mafia husband, whose leg was in a large boot cast. The room was painted a dark shade of red. All of the dining room. Communist Russia. The lighting was low as well, making for an almost sultry effect. This wasn't lessened, either, by the full bar in the corner.

The bar was where Rick made himself comfortable. He offered me a drink. I declined as I sat at the table, choosing a spot nearest the door to the hall and entryway. I was eager for Mrs. Means to come in. I could hear some commotion around the corner where the kitchen must have been.

"So, you wanna be a history teacher, huh?" Rick said as he popped open a bottle of clear liquor, pouring it in a glass over his ice cubes.

"Um, yes," I said, crossing my legs under the table. "I've always loved old stuff, I guess."

"I'll bet you have," he said with a smirk.

Maybe that was the wrong thing to say. It was one of my go-to responses, why I liked history. I really did like ancient things. I dreamed of my future house being full of antiques, not red walls, bars, and East-Asian-inspired art. *Is Mrs. Means a closeted Buddhist?*

Thankfully, Mrs. Means came around the corner with what looked to be a casserole dish.

"Hi, Rachel!" she said warmly, with more enthusiasm than she ever used to teach ancient history. Her bright eyes made me more optimistic about this meal, along with the divine smell coming from the casserole dish. I couldn't remember the last time I had a homemade dish like this—I cooked, but only small things for myself. Never a full casserole meal.

"Thank you so much for having me. It's really nice to sit at a dining room table with people for once," I said, putting my napkin in my lap as Mrs. Means sat down across from me.

"What? You don't cook for your boyfriend?" Rick said, sitting at the head of the table, clear drink in hand. Because I had forgone an alcoholic drink, it looked like I'd be thirsty with my meal. Mrs. Means had poured herself a glass of red wine.

My face must have been as red as it felt, because Mrs. Means shot her husband a chastising look that said, "Don't interrogate our guest about her love life!" or maybe "Hey, old fart, this is the twenty-first century. We don't expect women to cook for their men anymore!"

As I always did with uncomfortable questions, I aimed for being diplomatic and kind, hoping to avoid any awkward follow-up questions.

"Oh no, no boyfriend, but I don't have much time to cook for myself these days anyway. College and student teaching keeps me pretty busy. I hardly have time for a social life."

Mrs. Means took the opportunity to steer the conversation in the direction she wanted, giving me advice about how to be social early in my career. How to build the right connections and create relationships.

Dinner passed pleasantly enough, with Rick keeping his mouth shut while he ate, all of us using decent table manners and decorum, speaking only once we were done swallowing, dabbing our mouths with our napkins. Mrs. Means did have some class to her, I'll give her that.

Her husband, not so much.

After dinner, which was absolutely delicious, Mrs. Means quickly cleared the table and again offered me a drink. When I declined yet another offer of alcohol, she changed her offer to tea.

"I have some great Earl Grey we got last time we were in England. I'll brew some for you."

I didn't have the chance or room to turn her down again before she turned around the corner to brew the tea. I only hoped I wasn't left to converse with Rick the entire time. We were still seated at the table when he angled his chair toward me and said, "You like hot tubs?"

An odd turn of conversation, but if it was something he was interested in discussing, then I could play along.

"I mean, yeah, I guess so. I haven't been in them often."

"Ahh. I love my hot tub. I would sit in it every night if I could. It's really too fucking bad I can't use it right now with my leg and all." He nodded to his leg, casted up to his knee.

"Oh, right, I'm sorry about your leg. How is it feeling?" I asked, trying to keep him talking.

"Oh, it's fine. We could go out back on the deck and use the hot tub tonight if you wanted. I could turn it on for you. I could just watch," he said with no degree of shame or discomfort.

I gulped but tried not to give him the satisfaction of looking uncomfortable. "Oh, I didn't bring a swimsuit. Thank you, though."

His sultry gaze let me know that me without a swimsuit would be no problem for him. "Shame," he said simply.

I squirmed, waiting for Mrs. Means to return from the kitchen.

As soon as she came through the door, mugs in hand, I stood from my seat.

"I better be going. It's getting late. Thank you so much for dinner," I said as I moved toward the door.

Mrs. Means had the courtesy of looking concerned. She glanced from me to her husband, something flashing in her face in a way that made me think she was familiar with how her husband could be. Maybe he always treated young women this way.

I didn't wait for her to say anything as I turned and walked toward the door, grabbing my jacket and slinging it on in a fluid movement. The closer I was to leaving, the closer I felt to crying.

I wasn't even sure why.

Why did a man objectifying me make me feel like crying? It's not like he *did* anything. It's not like he touched me. The casserole was turning in my stomach.

I was barely out the door before I felt the lump rise in my throat. I heard Mrs. Means calling her goodbyes behind me, but I was already gone. I got down the front steps and into my car without looking back, and I left tire marks on the pristine curb as I screeched away.

Tears were running down my face, and my chest was tight as I found my way out of the fancy neighborhood.

I was back to my house and parked in the alleyway when I pulled my phone out of my jacket pocket, wishing I'd kept it closer, in my hand, in case I'd needed to call anyone. I felt anger, though I knew it was mostly unfounded, at myself for being in a situation where I felt so nervous.

But anger isn't always rational, and I could never convince my brain to overpower my heart.

"Hey." Luke picked up on the second ring, sounding frustrated but chipper. "How the hell do you complete this assignment for Josephine's class?"

It almost made me smile to hear his voice, hear how utterly concerned he was with something that was so menial to me right now.

"I don't know. I'll help you with it this weekend. Hey, listen, something really weird just happened to me, and I want to tell someone about it," I said as I sat in my car.

"Yeah, what's up?" he asked. I could hear music playing in the background. He always had music playing, which was way distracting to me, but I guess it helped him work.

I told him all about the encounter with Rick. I told Luke that I'd give Rick the benefit of the doubt, and maybe he didn't intend to make me uncomfortable, but regardless I felt gross and was just glad to get out of there.

"Well, you are pretty hot, so he's not wrong." He laughed.

I cringed. I know he was trying to help by making me laugh, but I definitely needed something stronger to make me feel better.

When I didn't say anything, he continued, "Are you worried? Like, he didn't touch you or anything, right?"

"No, God no, but it just made me really upset and I needed to vent."

"Rachel, if you're actually worried, maybe you should tell Josephine. That could be a real cause for concern with the program to give you a cooperating teacher like that." His mood had shifted from playful to something else I couldn't place over the phone. Irritation? Maybe he was just concerned for me.

"No, no, it's fine. I don't need to do that. I'll be okay. Thanks for listening, though," I said quickly, feeling stupid for complaining to a man who could never understand.

"Okay, Rachel. You should tell Josephine if you're worried, but whatever," he said abruptly.

I didn't tell Josephine. I never told another person. And Mrs. Means never mentioned it.

I didn't need another thing to make a fuss over.

CHAPTER TWENTY-TWO

MY TWENTY-SECOND BIRTHDAY came and nearly went with little to no excitement. As it was the last week of the term before spring break, I knew that everyone at school was tense. Not the middle schoolers, though; they were going crazy, ready to break out. The anticipation was palpable. Mrs. Means would be heading on a cruise to Cancun with her hot-tub-loving husband. I would be here.

My birthday fell on a Tuesday this year, so I had Jared's class. Lucie had wished me a happy birthday when I saw her in between student teaching and night class, and she gave me a quick hug before she was out the door, onto wherever she went all the time.

Grandma called while I was teaching. I hadn't had the chance to call her back before I had to head to Jared's class. I was really trying not to think about the fact that Luke hadn't texted me once that day. I'd hoped in vain that he would remember my birthday, as I knew his. It was just a few weeks away—mid-April.

When Luke didn't even sit by me, I felt like such a foolish, naive idiot. He sat at the table behind mine, next to Adam, while I was at our usual table at the front with Sarah and a few other people who were completely ignorant of the significance of the day for me. As Jared went on and on about understanding basic phonics of multiple world languages, I felt more and more alone.

I felt stupid for getting my hopes up that anyone would even remember me during such a stressful time for everyone. No one usually did anything for my birthday—why should this year be any different? Last night I baked myself a cake. I loved the tradition of cake on birthdays. I stayed up late after class and baked the cake, letting it cool overnight before frosting it.

Lucie honestly seemed a little pissed—saying she would have made me one if I asked. I somehow doubted that. Besides, I didn't want to have to ask to be celebrated.

Jared dismissed the class. No singing, no anything. I was ready to head home to frost my own cake and host my own pity party when I felt familiar breathy lips behind my ear.

"Happy birthday," Luke said, breathing as he leaned into my back, for only a brief moment; then he stepped away. He had slid a brown paper bag, the type alcoholics used to wrap their liquor in public, next to my hand on the table. I turned around in time to see him give me a smirk and a cute wink over his shoulder as he walked away.

I peered in the bag.

Though it wasn't specially wrapped, my heart was about to burst, if only at the mere fact that Luke remembered. That someone got me something.

There, at the bottom of the crumpled paper bag, was a can of Pepsi, a chocolate bar, and a note. I didn't pull out the note. I wanted to wait until I got home.

Luke and Adam had already walked off, so I hurried home by myself, clutching the paper bag close to me in the dark. As soon as I got through the door and found the house empty, I pulled the handwritten note out of the bag and scanned it. It was a poem. A limerick, by Luke, by the looks of it. It read:

> The cutest girl in the cohort
> Likes to hang out with the tall dork.
> It's her birthday today.
> I wanted to say hey
> And tell her how special she is; I want to see her more and more every day.
> (I'm bad at poetry.)

My eyes welled with tears at the thoughtfulness of the gift. He did suck at poetry, but he was really something.

I smiled the entire time I frosted my birthday cake. As much as I would hate to admit to anyone, I sang the "Happy Birthday" song to myself and blew out a scented candle I lit for the occasion. I didn't have birthday candles, but I figured any candle would do.

I ate a single piece of funfetti cake with sprinkles, then cleaned up the kitchen, stowing the rest of the cake for breakfast tomorrow.

As I got into bed that night, the first night I was twenty-two, a harrowing thought crossed my mind: Why couldn't Luke wish me a happy birthday out loud? Why did he pass me my gift in such a stealthy way, then walk away without so much as a hug? Was he hiding me from Adam, or anyone else? Ivy's face flashed in my mind as I pictured him hiding me in a dark room while he stood in the light with everyone else.

I couldn't let my mind go there. Not tonight. Especially since I hadn't texted or called to thank him either. No, I would just be happy with my consumable gifts, which seemed too special to eat or drink, and the cute poem he'd written.

I took a deep breath and forced myself to smile up at the ceiling of my bedroom.

But I still couldn't sleep that night. My thoughts were occupied by insincere poems, raised handguns, and broken promises.

CHAPTER TWENTY-THREE

I CALLED GRANDMA BACK the next day, and it felt unbelievably good to hear her voice.

I asked her about the weather in Arizona, and she told me about her new Bunco club. She asked me how everything was for me, and I said fine. If she thought anything was wrong, she didn't mention it. I missed her terribly. But I didn't want to bring her down with my negativity, and I didn't want to worry her.

After all, I was fine. I was pushing through. I was going to be okay.

I sent Luke a text to thank him for the gifts. I felt a little puzzled after our short interaction yesterday, not to mention after my bout of overthinking last night. *Thanks for the gift last night. That was really, really sweet of you.*

He replied quickly, despite being at his own school. *I hope you had a happy birthday. Pizza Friday?*

Terse, but to the point, I guess. My response was similar. *Yeah, sounds great.*

I tried to imagine brushing him off my shoulder like a piece of lint, but I could still feel the weight on me. I felt heavy. And alone.

The rest of the week went as smoothly as the week before a break can go with middle schoolers. We had hit my target and wrapped up our study of the Byzantines before the end of March, moving onto the Ottoman Turks, to be continued after spring break. The most promising part to me was that I only had about six more weeks of student teaching left; then I would receive my degree, my teaching license, and hopefully the kickass letter of recommendation Mrs. Means kept dangling over me. I was beyond ready to apply for jobs.

I still made a habit of checking every other day for postings. Still not much.

I wasn't too worried about it. I knew there'd be a lot more postings over spring break. Maybe I'd use some of my free time alone to work on my application materials. Lucie would be gone—her family was taking her on a trip to Seattle.

Still, I was a little worried that the loneliness of break might swallow me. I envisioned the ground beneath me as a large, hungry worm, opening his mouth wider and wider, hoping I might fall in, his slimy lips closing around me.

No, I couldn't be afraid. I'd spent most of my life alone, emotionally at least. I was tough.

My thoughts had kind of been spiraling this week, ever since my birthday. My feelings toward Luke were more complicated than ever. I was looking forward to our pizza date, though. I figured maybe I'd get some clarity. In my head, I was calling our pizza thing a date, because since we'd kissed, I figured we were something of an item. At least more than friends. My heart would break if he called me just a friend.

Once again, during Annabel's class, Luke made no mention to anyone else at our table about our dinner plans. He didn't give me direct attention during class, sitting on the opposite side of the round table, torturously near but too far. Maybe he was giving himself space to maintain his thoughts, and sitting next to me would be too distracting. I felt his foot brush against mine under the table a few times, but I resisted petting his leg back in case it was someone else's foot by mistake.

After class, I got my things together in my bag promptly, not trying to linger after everyone left. I wanted to see if he would leave with me right away or if he would hang back until others left. I was analyzing his every move. Which is not an easy way to live.

Of course, I was left standing there awkwardly while Luke held conversations with nearly everyone around our tables, until we all filed out together. Some people made for their cars, bikes, or the bus stop, while we set off on foot toward Rodeo's.

I liked that Rodeo's had become our spot.

We didn't talk very much as we walked. We both had our dark hoods up against the rain, and we walked most of the way single file to let partygoers pass us by. I walked in front of him until we reached the warmth radiating from the inside of Rodeo's.

I ordered for us and paid, getting us our same respective orders (me, one slice of pepperoni and a Pepsi, him a beer and two slices of the crap with mushrooms and olives all over it). They asked to see my ID for his beer. I'd never seen them ask him, and I figured I was becoming somewhat of a regular, but whatever. Maybe one day I'd be flattered to be carded.

He didn't say anything more about my birthday, about the gift, or how he'd gone about giving it to me. I didn't bring it up either. I liked to keep it light with Luke. I felt like if I became too serious for him, he'd slip away.

We'd just gotten our pizza when he took a bite and said, while chewing, "So I wanted to talk to you about something. Last time we were here, you were telling me all about your trauma, like with your parents and stuff, and I wanted to tell you more about me and my experiences."

I was caught off guard. Here I was, thinking I had to keep it light, and he wants to tell me about the worst parts of his life. Never mind the fact that he thought what I told him before about my upbringing was me dumping my trauma on him. What happened with my mom and dad wasn't the most traumatic part of my life, by far. At least, it wasn't now. Maybe a few years back, like when I wrote my college admissions essay.

I wished I could go back to my state of mind then.

Before he went on, he reached across the table to grab my hand again. My heart leaped, but I was also nervous. What was he going to say, and would it change anything?

He went on, "I want to tell you about it because it really tore me apart. And I've been kind of damaged ever since."

Oh God. Had he been through something like I'd been through? The idea almost made me happy—in the most selfish way—that at least someone else could understand.

But that's not what he said. I nodded encouragingly, even though he was driving me crazy with anticipation. He knew it too.

"My last girlfriend, when I first came here to Big Bend, cheated on me. But she would never admit it."

I blinked in surprise, and then I swallowed my disappointment. A part of me felt empathetic.

"That's awful. How do you know she cheated if she wouldn't admit to it?" I asked, genuinely curious but also not sure what else to say.

"Well, I guess I can't know for a fact that she cheated while we were together, but she was always really close with my friend, Jason. Then, out of nowhere, she broke up with me, and almost immediately, she was dating him. So I know they had something going on behind my back. It destroyed me."

He was so sincere. It was reassuring to know that I wasn't the naivest person in the world.

"You must have really loved her, huh?" I asked, mostly wondering if he was entirely over it. Maybe it was a bad idea to start up with a guy who had unresolved issues from a past relationship.

I had conflicting feelings, both relieved and discouraged, when he said, "Eh. She was cool, but it was just hard losing them both at once, you know? It wasn't long after that that I moved back in with my parents, and then I got arrested. You know that whole story. Did you ever try to look up my mugshot?"

I had, but I wasn't going to admit that to his smug ass. I laughed it off, though I didn't particularly find the drunken behavior funny.

"So tell me about your family then. They accepted you back in after you moved out? They must live close by."

"Oh yeah," he said, dropping my hand and completely changing his demeanor. He was back to his usual cocky self. "My folks live about forty-five minutes up the road. I could never move too far from them. I'm really close with my family. They'll all be here in a big hoard for graduation, I'm sure. Have you sent out your graduation announcements yet? I'm so far behind, my mom is getting pissed."

I didn't want to tell him that I didn't have any to send out. The only person who really cared or knew that I was even in school was Grandma, and she knew when graduation was. She just wouldn't be traveling from Arizona for it.

The only reason I even planned on walking in the graduation ceremony was because of the camaraderie of my cohort, and I wasn't going to miss out on graduating all together with them. I had already purchased the overpriced cap and gown from the student store.

No, I didn't want him to compare my family situation to his, and I didn't want him thinking I was too damaged to be a family-oriented woman. I knew it was silly, but one of my biggest fears was people judging me for a situation out of my control. So I settled for a lie by omission.

"I can help you, if you want. I can help address envelopes and stuff. What are you doing over break?" I said, avoiding his question. I knew he wouldn't point it out, though. He never pointed out when I didn't answer his questions. I liked that about Luke, but sometimes it meant that I really had to speak up if I wanted him to know anything about me.

"I was going to spend a couple days up at my parents' house. You're not going home or on a trip or anything?" he asked, almost incredulously.

"No, I'll be staying here," I said. "So I'm totally available if you want to work on anything." We really didn't have schoolwork to catch up on or even get ahead on over spring break. The only thing I'd be getting ahead on were lesson plans, which Mrs. Means could still change on me at any time, so it wasn't really worth spending a ton of time on.

He seemed to consider this for a moment, which was a little unsettling. He was usually so impulsive. He spoke immediately after someone was finishing their sentence, not seeming to have to consider much at all. To have him look contemplative was unusual.

He sat back in his seat and crossed his arms before he said, "Why don't you come to my parents for a day? You can see where I grew up, and if my mom sees you addressing graduation announcements, she'll love you forever."

I lit up at his words. I wondered if he knew the impact it had on me, teasing that someone could love me forever. They were the exact words I needed to hear to be ensnared. Like a trap set only for Rachel.

So it was settled. On Monday morning, Luke would come get me in his little car, and we'd drive thirty miles north to see his parents. I would spend the day addressing envelopes, or whatever he needed me to do, while I charmed his mom into convincing her son to make me his girlfriend. Or something like that.

After he walked me home that night, I couldn't stop thinking about a revelation I'd had earlier.

I was thinking about fears.

I was thinking about how I was aware for a long time that I was afraid of being judged for my homelife. I didn't want people to think I was rough around the edges, or that I'd be messed up psychologically for my upbringing. After all, everyone had trauma; they either claimed it or ignored it. Even Luke, who maybe carried trust issues.

I got that, but there was something nagging at me ever since I avoided talking about going home for spring break. I hadn't wanted him to judge me for what I'd been through, but I also hadn't wanted to seem whiny about it. I didn't want to come across like I was looking for handouts. I didn't think Luke did either, but he still opened up to me about what bothered him about his past.

My feelings about my tumultuous upbringing were the same as my feelings about my student-teaching career. I didn't want to overshare those feelings, because I didn't want them to pity me or judge me for whining.

I wanted to be tough and brave. That image obviously mattered to me above a lot of things, even opening myself up to connect with another person. How was I any different? I judged Luke for being so suave, smooth, claiming no one could see beneath the surface.

I felt like I was seeing myself in a different light—the way others saw me. I had these feelings and thoughts swirling beneath the surface, feeling like I could explode. There was too much going on in my heart and head. I imagined that people saw me as pensive and deep, but how could they if I kept it all in? I fear I seem demure, quiet, shy, reserved, standoffish.

I used to think I knew myself. Maybe I did. But maybe I'd changed.

CHAPTER TWENTY-FOUR

MY WEEKEND WAS spent in anticipation of my family date with Luke and the Earnests on Monday. Lucie left Saturday morning with her parents, so I had two whole days of solitude to fret over what to wear and how to act, obsessing over whether I would fall in love with this family and never want to leave.

I completed every monotonous task I could think of to keep myself busy. I cleaned the apartment from top to bottom, even dusting the baseboards and scrubbing the shower. I snaked the shower drain and pulled out gobs of Lucie's long black hair. I gagged.

I baked cookies from scratch and went grocery shopping. I kept myself from thinking too much about anything—until night came. When I laid in bed, staring at the ceiling, I could only think about my students' faces when we heard gunshots in the building.

Monday morning came at last, and I was dressed and ready an hour before Luke said he'd come get me. I elected to wear jeans—my nicest jeans—with the boots I bought the day after the incident. With the weird spring weather, which sometimes felt like winter and sometimes felt like summer, I decided layers were the best way to go. So I had on a T-shirt underneath an open button-down and a light jacket.

I even curled my hair.

He'd never come to the door of my apartment—the couple of times he walked me home, he stopped by the lamppost in the alley—so I came out to meet him at his car and climbed into the passenger seat. His car was exactly what I would expect from him: a decade-old sedan with paint chipping off one panel.

He greeted me with a quick kiss on the lips.

It made me wonder if he was introducing me to his family as a friend or something more. I was remarkably calm as we drove north on the freeway, then switched off onto a country road, toward the little town of Allsbury.

As we approached the small town center, Luke turned down the music to point out some of his favorite local places. We passed by his high school and the pizza place he worked at before exiting out the other side of the main town area and toward his family's home.

I couldn't help but look around and wonder whether it was here, in the middle of his picturesque hometown, that he'd been arrested.

He didn't have to point out his parents' house. I knew which one it was—it was adorable. I loved it.

In fact, I liked the look of this entire town. It was the kind of place I could see myself living—not too big, not too small. It had some restaurants and culture, but it was calm and slow.

But his family's house . . . I was absolutely in love.

With a wide raised porch and craftsman details, the white house was on the edge of a neighborhood that ended with a tree-lined hillside. With the mature fruit trees in the front yard and perfectly mown grass, the house looked to be nearly 100 years old. Though the property itself was small, it was the exact type of street people dreamed of raising a family on. The kind where kids could ride their bikes, and you could ask a neighbor for some milk or sugar.

In short, it was my dream house. And the tall, dark-haired woman stepping out onto the porch could be my dream mother-in-law.

Marissa turned out to be a wonderful woman. After greeting us, giving Luke a huge hug and me a small one, she unloaded the giant laundry basket from Luke's trunk and ushered us into the house, where she'd baked the most delicious banana bread, littered with cinnamon and chocolate chips.

She mostly talked to Luke, and he to her, but I chipped in a bit about school and student teaching. She didn't seem that interested in me, but maybe that was because Luke hadn't introduced me with any title. It wasn't "This is Rachel, my girlfriend," or "This is Rachel, my friend"; it was just "This is Rachel." So why would she be invested in learning about me?

Despite the feeling of being unclaimed by Luke as anything, I was enjoying myself. It felt unbelievably nice to be out of Big Bend, out where it was quiet and the only human noises were our voices. No sirens, no helicopters.

We were sitting on the back porch, rocking in chairs side by side, the spring breeze rustling my hair, when I began to daydream, absorbing the peace and serenity of my surroundings.

It would be amazing to live in a place like this. I could teach at a small-town high school, and be a part of the community. Find comfort in the silence. I envisioned that life for myself.

I could see myself being a teacher that students felt comforted by, and safe with, and I could advise extracurricular clubs for history buffs, LGBTQ+ students, or a meditation club. I could see myself running down to the local pizza place on a Friday night when I didn't want to cook and telling the young person behind the counter that my husband used to work there when he was a teen.

I could imagine coming to Marissa and Frank's house for Thanksgiving dinner, having them accept me as one of their own, and they'd love my grandma too. She'd be welcome whenever she could make it.

I almost cried at the thought of it all.

Luke's mom's voice broke me from my stupor. She'd taken a break from telling Luke the latest gossip about people I didn't know to ask me a question. I glanced at Luke for help, not having registered what she said. He raised his eyebrows. I realized she had asked me where I was hoping to land a job after graduation.

"Oh. I'm not sure yet! I'm open to going anywhere, if the job is a good fit. I'd really like a smaller community. The size of Allsbury actually looks about perfect," I said, gazing at Luke. His hazel eyes lifted to mine. That seemed to satisfy Marissa because she smiled at me and began detailing how she had fallen in love with Allsbury—and how it was a great place to raise kids.

We spent the afternoon addressing envelopes. I'd never had phenomenal, cutesy, feminine handwriting, but it was certainly better than Luke's, so I was the designated addresser. He tucked graduation invites into the envelopes, then sealed and stamped them. I caught Marissa grinning every time she passed by us at the dining room table.

Luke wasn't kidding—he had dozens upon dozens of graduation announcements to send out. My social circle was nothing in comparison.

The Earnests were the type of family I would have dreamed to find myself in. Marissa and Frank had been married for nearly thirty years, they had a beautiful home, and they were close with their sons. However, when Frank made it home that evening, I could see how he and Luke really butted heads. They were entirely too similar—the dark curls (though Franks were streaked with gray), the hazel eyes, and the temper. Frank's arrival cut our visit short, and Luke was ready to go by the time it was getting dark.

I thanked the Earnests profusely for their hospitality, hoping I might be invited back soon. I yearned for that kind of family dynamic. Even with the tension, maybe even the dysfunction at times, I wanted that life for myself. The only thing in my way? Luke.

I wasn't sure if he was on board with the whole thing.

As he shut his driver-side door and we started pulling away from the dream visit, he smiled.

"While you were in the bathroom, my mom asked me about ten times why we're not dating."

I hesitated a beat before saying, "And what'd you tell her?"

He just shook his head and smiled.

CHAPTER TWENTY-FIVE

I WAS PRETTY NEARLY in love with Luke. He occupied all my thoughts, outside of the pressures of student teaching and finding a job. We'd spent another day together during spring break, on the hunt for jobs to apply for. We'd stayed up late watching a movie and cuddling close.

At one point we'd had a pretty steamy make-out session, and I let him get my top off entirely, but I still wasn't ready to give all of myself to him.

I wasn't sure why, really. I'd never had sex with someone I wasn't officially dating, and maybe I was just waiting for him to declare some more solid feelings for me. But maybe Luke wasn't the kind of guy who needed to verbally express things, and I should take his actions above his words. His actions showed he felt the same way about me too.

We were an item in our hearts, even if the rest of the world wasn't aware of it yet.

And they certainly weren't aware of it.

The next week, Luke was having a party. His birthday party. At his house. He invited everyone in our cohort—it was to take place after class on Friday night.

Thankfully, the last term of classes didn't include Annabel or Jared as my professors. I was relieved to be rid of them. Instead, now we met as a cohort on Monday and Friday nights, basically to assess our student-teaching skills and complete our paperwork for our teaching licenses. A piece of cake, in comparison to the last two terms.

So, after he announced to the cohort on Monday that he'd be hosting his own birthday party on Friday, I was a little nervous. First of all, I didn't really enjoy parties. But mostly it was that I had no idea how Luke would act around me in front of everyone, especially in such cozy quarters.

I was also bummed that this was taking the place of our Friday night pizza time. But hey, how often does a guy turn twenty-four?

Friday came, and I was without a plan, an outfit, or a gift. I asked Lucie what I should get for a guy in my cohort. She said beer. When I explained that I wanted something a little more meaningful, hinting that I liked this guy, like *really* liked this guy, she seemed confused.

"Luke, the guy who I said was like the golden boy of our cohort? He loves the attention on him?"

There were no signs of recognition on her face as she furrowed her brow, maybe trying to remember. She seemed unimpressed and didn't offer any other gift ideas.

Golden boy, indeed, when we sang to him in class, as directed by Josephine. We hadn't sung a birthday song to anyone all year, and yet we did for Luke. I didn't feel jealous, though. I felt excited for him. He didn't blush, but he put on an abashed face and a smirk, shaking his head as if to say, *Who, me? No way. I was not expecting this.*

I went with the beer idea for a gift, which I would grab on my way home before the party. I didn't want to get just any beer, though, especially since I didn't know a thing about different beers, but I had an idea in mind.

I said my quick goodbyes after class, saying I'd see them in a bit.

I nearly ran through the convenience store down the street, then dropped my school stuff off at home. Since it was already late, I wanted to get going.

I chose not to change my clothes. Everyone had already seen me in my student-teaching outfit, and I didn't want to seem like I was trying too hard. Besides, casual Friday meant I was wearing jeans with a cute, casual top anyway.

I tucked the single beer bottle on the inside pocket of my jacket and walked the dark few blocks toward Luke's.

It was a college-boy house party for sure. All the lights were on as I walked up, I could hear the music from the street, and there were people sitting on the front steps, exhaling clouds of smoke. Pot, from the smell of it.

I suddenly felt very out of place, just like I feared I would. Would I fit in with all the other people in Luke's life?

I stepped up the stairs, past the smokers, barely acknowledging them, as I pushed into the house. It was full of people, and the lights were dim. The music was loud, and I began to get anxious. I felt on edge as my eyes searched for anyone I knew.

I walked through the crowded living room, into the kitchen, where the dining table I sat at the night of our first kiss was covered in liquor bottles and Solo cups, some of which had clearly spilled. Everything looked sticky.

What a nightmare this would be to clean up tomorrow.

In the kitchen, I was happy to find Sarah and Briseyda, both with cups in their hands but clearly not drunk yet. I sidled up to them, relieved that they, too, were in their school clothes. That was until a couple of beautiful young women came over to assess us.

"Hey, do you want something to drink?" one of them asked, as if she was the host. I took her in: all five-foot-nine of her. She towered over me, with her long dark hair that grazed below the hemline of her barely-there shirt. Inches of skin showed above her navel. She was thin in the way that nineteen-year-olds are thin—like their body hasn't caught up with them yet. Not skinny in the way that I was skinny, like I was losing weight from being too busy to eat.

I tried to look up at her level. "Yeah, please. Whatever is easiest," I said. She quickly went over to the defiled kitchen table and poured some mystery liquids into a cup for me. I watched her the whole time, looking to see how comfortable she was in Luke's space. Was she dating one of Luke's roommates?

She brought back my cup and handed it to me, and I offered my sincerest thanks.

"Oh my God, I love your outfit," she said to Briseyda, "You all look like you came out of an Ann Taylor catalog!" Her friend stifled a snorted laugh.

Maybe this girl was drunk, but did she have to be so bitchy? I wasn't supposed to say bitchy, as it was a derogatory term used to oppress women, but it was all that was in my head. Bitchy, bitchy, bitchy.

I pictured her like a mean cheerleader in a cliché movie, and we were the nerds she was being mean to in a backhanded way. But Briseyda just said, "Thanks."

"Who are you?" I asked, trying to make it sound condescending.

"Oh, I'm Amber," she said, "and this is Chloe." She nodded to her friend.

"Okay, well, I'll let you know if I need another drink," I said dismissively. She seemed unbothered as she walked into the crowded living room with her friend in tow.

"What a little bitch!" Briseyda said after she'd left. Sarah and I exchanged a glance before we busted up laughing.

"I mean it!" Briseyda said, though she was smiling too. "Who does that little brat think she is? That was such a burn! I feel more insulted than I do when my middle school students say things like that. Because she knows what she's doing by saying that."

"Who even is she, anyway?" I asked, probing to see if they knew how she was connected to Luke.

And then the man himself appeared. Looking sexy as hell in a fitted black T-shirt and jeans. I'd seen Luke at ease in the comfort of his own home, but tonight, with all the attention on him, and clearly already bordering on intoxicated, he breezed in with a swaggering confidence that looked fantastic on him.

"Thanks for coming!" he said loudly as he wrapped his arms around Sarah and Briseyda. I may have bristled, but I quickly thought better of saying anything. Was he testing me? Trying to tease me? What was his game?

Luckily, I had a trick up my sleeve too. Or rather, in my jacket.

"Happy birthday." I attempted my most charming smile as I opened my jacket and pulled the single beer bottle out of my interior pocket. "It's a blond ale, because I know how much you enjoy blonds."

Sarah gaped, but Luke gave me his most attractive smile as he let go of their shoulders to embrace me. "Thank you," he said into my hair, then leaned into my neck. "You look really fucking hot, by the way. But I really think you're more of a mousy brunette than a blond."

My heart leaped in my chest, and my cheeks heated, even if I was disgusted at the thought of looking anything like a mouse.

"I'm going to open this right now!" he announced loudly before seeing someone else to talk to and leaving me with Sarah and Briseyda.

He spent most of the night running from group to group, being the loyal host, I suppose. I spent most of my night waiting for a chance to talk to him, be alone with him. Wondering if he might have me stay the night.

I was sitting on the living room couch with some cohort people when Daniel, the cohort comrade student teaching down the road from me, approached with a beer in his hand, though he was already drunk. I, however, had sipped at whatever the hell Amber made me without too much of a buzz coming on. It had grown warm in my hand.

Daniel plopped down on the couch next to me, and I knew it was intentional that he came to me. I could sense that he had something to say to me, his eyes focused on me when he stepped into the room; then he made a beeline toward me. I tried in vain to brace myself.

"Rachel," he said with sorrow in his eyes, "I've been wanting to talk to you about the whole shooting thing." My heart stopped. I felt my insides tighten. No, no, no. I couldn't talk about this here. Not now. I looked around for an escape, but he seemed intent as he continued on.

"Because, like, nobody really knows but us, because we know about it, and how fucked up it all was. And it is! And how the people out there with signs and stuff, it's such bullshit." He was slurring his words, and they were coming out somewhat incoherently, but I got the point. He was hurting too. And he couldn't talk about it sober.

"And, like, I know it had to have messed you up. I know you were right there. And you look like you just gotta be, like, so brave." He burped. "But, like, if you need to talk about it at all, like, ever, you can talk to me. Because I know." He looked at me deeply, and I knew he meant it, but he was the one who seemed like he needed to talk about it.

"Thanks, Daniel," I said sincerely. "I wouldn't wish it on anyone, but I'm glad that you know what it's been like for me. Thank you for acknowledging it."

And I did feel grateful. But I also felt like I'd been punched in the stomach, and I needed to either cry or throw up. At that moment, Luke brought in a bottle of Crown Royal whiskey.

"Who wants shots?" he said drunkenly and loudly.

"Ew, I cannot do Crown," Sarah said.

It was mostly the boys who stood up enthusiastically. Maybe it was because it was Luke holding the bottle, maybe it was because

I was always the girl in the boy's club of social studies, or maybe it was because of this conversation with Daniel, but I jumped up too.

I took one shot, then two. And by then, everything was a blur. After the initial rounds, everyone was passing the bottle around, taking swigs until it was gone.

One minute I was sitting on the couch; then I blinked, and Sarah was giggling in my ear about how she had wiped up some pee that someone had left all over the toilet seat because she thought it'd be nice. She was too nice for her own good.

Then I blinked again, and I was in a corner with Luke, his tongue tickling my earlobe as he whispered in my ear, a new beer in his hand that was draped around my shoulder, the condensation dripping onto my shirt, giving me chills. No one was paying us any mind as he went on and on in my ear, saying, "And if we both got jobs near here, then we could even live together after graduation."

Daniel was crying as someone put him in an Uber to get him home.

Briseyda was dancing on the coffee table.

Jack was playing a guitar.

Bitchy Amber was smoking with Luke's roommates.

I was leaving to go home alone through the dark.

The last thing I noticed at Luke's was the half-empty bottle of blond ale sitting on the counter, forgotten.

CHAPTER TWENTY-SIX

I WAS EVEN SICKER this time than last time. I had to get up before morning just to throw up, and I met Lucie in the bathroom. She wasn't puking, but she was sitting on the bathroom floor in her underwear and a T-shirt. Waiting to puke. She was coherent, so we elected to share the bathroom while we both took turns leaning over the toilet.

"I think I might have some kind of alcohol intolerance," I said between gags, my head nearly in the toilet bowl. "Every time I've had even a little to drink in the last couple of months, I've had these horrible reactions and felt like crap." I wretched again, my back muscles straining.

"Yeah, could be," Lucie said. "What have you been drinking? Maybe you're allergic to something in it."

I contemplated that while I wiped my mouth and flushed the toilet.

"Where'd you go tonight?" Lucie asked while we both sat against the wall opposite the toilet.

"It was Luke's birthday party—the guy I got the beer for. He invited a bunch of cohort people, but there were a ton of other people there too. He's really social."

"Luke... what's he look like again?" she asked, genuinely racking her brain for some memory or image to attach him to.

"Luke's the tall one with the curly dark hair? The social studies guy?"

"Is he the one still dating his high school sweetheart?" she asked.

"No, that's Adam. Luke's single. Well, kind of. I've kind of been seeing him. I'm not really sure what we are, actually, especially not after tonight."

She looked genuinely astonished. "Okay, okay, back up. First of all, you've been dating someone? Since when? Has he been over here?"

"No, he hasn't come over here ever. We mostly hang out at his place or go out. We've been going out every week since January." I trailed off, not knowing what else to say. Especially when she was looking at me so incredulously.

I almost thought she was going to yell at me, and I wasn't sure if she was mad because of the man in question or because of how long it had been without her knowing. Especially when she said, "Isn't that the guy you used to make fun of for being all fake and charming to people all the time? The one you called golden boy?"

I took a pause to lean over the toilet and gag until stomach bile rose up. I spit it into the toilet water, then flushed before leaning back next to Lucie.

"Um, yeah. He's still kind of that way, like he has a mask on for the world, but he's more genuine one-on-one. I could really see us being together long-term. We match so well."

She shook her head slightly. "Well. Just be careful, Rach. I don't want to see you get hurt. More."

I wanted to ask her what she meant by that last part, but she made to get up.

"Kay, I'm going to bed. If you hear me get back up to puke, mind your own business. We'll rendezvous for Gatorade tomorrow. Love ya," she said as she slipped out the door.

"Hey Luce," I called from where I was still squatted across from the toilet. She peeked her head back around the door frame. Maybe I was drunk and being overly affectionate, or maybe I just needed to let her know, but I said, "It was nice talking to you tonight. I missed you."

She smiled slightly, but it didn't reach her eyes. "Goodnight, Rach."

We both stayed in bed until noon the next day.

***

It felt like Mrs. Means was actually starting to trust me. She was giving me full control of her first four classes most days, so I taught up until lunch every day. We finally had a good dynamic going.

She would even leave the room while I was teaching, and I suspected that she didn't have anywhere to go but was trying to give me the space to feel like I was truly in charge. The students seemed to like my casual way of asking questions and inviting conversation, rather than insisting on only correct answers, and the classes I taught generally flowed smoothly.

On an innocuous Wednesday, a lot of things changed at once.

First of all, Mr. Tyler announced to the staff that he would be vacating the position at the end of the year. He was not shy to admit that it was because of the incident earlier this year and the pressures and chaos that it created for him. His mental health had taken a hit, he said, and continuing to work here would be awful for his mental well-being.

We understood. At least, *I* understood. Some of the staff had the nerve to scoff behind his back in the hallway. But this raised another issue. Really, not an issue, but a new source of anxiety for me.

His job would be posted soon. And student teachers in the school were usually at the top of the list to fill vacant positions, as they were already familiar and comfortable with the school community and setting.

All eyes looked to me. Even though he taught English and not social studies, I would be certified to teach both, and I could easily slide into the role. Everyone kept asking me if I was going to apply. I had no choice but to smile and tell them some noncommittal answer like "probably" or "we'll see when it's posted!"

I didn't have much time to contemplate it before everyone was expecting answers from me. Luckily, I had at least a few days until it was official and I'd have to fill out the application.

"Oh, isn't this great!" Mrs. Means mused. "They'll have to review all applications, of course, but you'll be a shoo-in."

I smiled without showing my teeth.

The second thing that happened on that Wednesday is that the protests outside, which had calmed down after spring break, had somehow escalated once again.

There were two large rival groups with signs on sticks, and they were getting increasingly aggressive toward one another.

It was just midway through second period when I heard the sirens approaching, which immediately made me freeze. The students looked at me with wide eyes, Mrs. Means nowhere to be found, when they made the announcement.

"Teachers, we are going on lockdown. Please secure all doors immediately." Even the office lady sounded extremely exhausted.

Please, no, no, no, not again was all I could think as my body moved unconsciously toward the door, bringing it closed while Mrs. Means appeared down the hallway, hustling toward me to get through the door before I locked it. My brain pictured her as Indiana Jones, flying under the stone wall before he lost his hat.

I closed the door right after her, and we began placing papers over the windows, just like last time. I turned off the lights and moved toward my desk in silence.

Like last time, we sat in terrified silence, listening for any information on what was happening. The students stayed in their seats.

Unlike last time, we only had to wait about half an hour before Mrs. Cairns got on the intercom to let everyone know that we were not in danger, but that the demonstrations outside had gotten out of hand and were being broken up by the police. They wanted to keep students contained and safe and out of view. We were permitted to proceed with calm activities, like playing games or showing movies.

I got a nice text from Daniel, checking in to see if I was okay. He'd heard we were locked down again. I sent him a quick message: *I'm okay. Thanks for checking*, with a smiley face. Daniel was a genuinely nice guy.

So, from 10 a.m. until midafternoon, we did nothing. I tried to teach the seventh graders the archaic game *heads up, seven up*, but they were not enthused. Mrs. Means put on cartoons for them again.

By the end of the afternoon, I couldn't stand one more minute of the fucking *Looney Toons*.

The third thing that happened on that Wednesday is that I slept with Luke. Even though we had only exchanged a few text messages and sidelong glances during the class week, I had my mind made up when I went to his house that afternoon.

I texted him as soon as I left Rocky Middle, grateful that this time my car wasn't taped off by crime scene investigation tape, and asked if he wanted to hang out this afternoon. He texted back almost immediately.

By the time I got home, I was changing into a cuter outfit, brushing my teeth, and slipping out the door. I'd gone for my favorite jeans that hugged my hips and butt and a soft, surpliced long-sleeved shirt that wrapped around my waist flatteringly.

I didn't even bother with a jacket or grabbing my school bag. A little cotton-candy-flavored lip gloss, and I was walking the six blocks to the scene of last weekend's party.

Luke and I didn't talk much that evening. As soon as I got through the door to his bedroom, he closed it, locked it, and his hands were on me. Wrapping around me, pulling me close, putting his mouth on mine, claiming my breath with his, backing me toward the bed.

I kicked my shoes off as he lowered me down on my back, leaning over me as we sank into the old mattress.

His hands roamed up and down my body, taking his time to familiarize himself with every inch of it, some of it more angular than curvy with the weight I'd lost this school year. He felt all the places I'd never let him touch.

I reached my hand out to do the same with him, but he grabbed my wrist when my hand was inches above where I aimed for, pinning it back up by my head.

He was clearly asserting that he would be the one in control here. I guess I could allow that. It felt good to not have to think about it as I let myself go.

Let myself fall completely into whatever it was he wanted with me.

Let him know that I was his, and I wanted whatever he would offer me.

CHAPTER TWENTY-SEVEN

I WOKE UP THE next morning feeling good, I think. I think that's what the feeling was. I felt good about how it had gone with Luke. I was happy with my choices. I hoped he was happy with his.

He didn't walk me home like he had the first night we kissed. It had grown chilly that night, and my low-cut top did little to protect me from shivering. I had vaguely asked to borrow a sweatshirt, but he said he didn't want to lend me something that he wasn't sure he'd get back. I felt the same way about my emotions.

I walked through the streets warily, nervously, almost waiting for a perpetrator to jump out of a shadow and harass me.

I was relieved to get home in one piece. Relief from the nerves, that's what I told myself I was feeling.

I couldn't remember the last time I'd smiled. I certainly hadn't tonight, even though everything had gone my way, hadn't it? I'd gotten exactly what I wanted, hadn't I?

I was repeating the same loop of thoughts in my head as I made my way into bed.

I'd wanted Luke for months now, and I'd finally let myself have him. I kept repeating that in my head, waiting to fall asleep. Just when I thought I'd warmed up, I started shivering again, ruminating again.

I didn't feel good about heading back out to Rocky Middle School. If I had a store of sick days to pull from, I might have taken that day off. But for student teaching, I had to reach my hours in time to get my license, so a day off wasn't in the cards.

I drove out in silence, staring through the windshield. Spring had sprung, and Big Bend was experiencing the most beautiful days of the year. I'd hardly noticed.

I was expecting the police this time when I pulled up. There were two police cars and half a dozen deputies standing outside the building. The students were being ushered in to wait for the first bell.

How much were these kids going to have to endure? I tried to small talk with them casually and calmly as I made my way through the crowd to Mrs. Means's room. They seemed all too used to the repeated fear they were experiencing.

Despite the stress, Mrs. Means seemed to be in a great mood.

"Hey," she said enthusiastically, "Mr. Tyler's job was posted this morning. I would apply as soon as you can today. Did you bring your computer? You could work on it this morning, and I can teach first period."

I was a little blindsided, a little surprised. Caught off guard. I hadn't given any thought last night to whether I would even want to apply, and now I was being pressured into applying right now. I was glad that I didn't have to think on my feet for a quick lie, because I never brought my computer with me. I was too paranoid about it getting stolen, and I couldn't afford to lose my schoolwork. Or afford to replace the computer.

"Oh, no I didn't bring my computer. I'll work on it tonight since I don't have class. I just need to get my application materials together.

Could you write me a letter of rec?"

It was the perfect set up. Now she would have to get a move on with writing me that letter if she wanted me as a coworker. It seemed to work.

"Oh yes, I will work on that this morning then. Sounds great! I'd just make sure to apply quickly because any job in Big Bend is a hot commodity."

I didn't want to say what I was thinking: that maybe after everything that had happened at Rocky this year, maybe a job *here* wouldn't be a "hot commodity." Still, I knew that the job wouldn't sit unfilled.

Living in Big Bend was the goal for a lot of people, even if it meant taking a shitty job at a shitty school in a shitty district with a history of gun violence and protests. Even if it meant working said shitty job for a lower salary than in more rural towns, just to be in the heart of the more urban area near the university and the nightlife.

Maybe I took living here for granted. But also, maybe I was ready to leave.

A conversation echoed in my mind, though, from last week. Luke said that we could live together here. I didn't think he meant as roommates—he meant as partners. He was dangling the life I desperately wanted in front of me like a carrot.

Did he know the impact those words would have on me, or was he oblivious to my deepest desires?

The thought was enough to have me searching for jobs in the area that afternoon when I got home.

The day of teaching went surprisingly well, given all the new negative excitement with the police. They stayed outside the school for the duration of the school day, monitoring and scaring off any protesters. I was relieved from their presence, for once.

When I got home, I immediately opened my computer to begin the renewed job search, comparing pay rates for rural districts versus urban ones and looking at what jobs were available around the state. Luke had said once that he'd planned to apply everywhere around the state in the hope that one school would want him.

Maybe I'd consider doing the same. Maybe we'd end up close to each other, at least. It didn't help that we were in direct competition with each other in the job market—I knew he wanted to teach high school social studies as well—and he was far more charming than I was. He'd get any job over me.

I applied for the job at Rocky, officially. Mrs. Means had given me a paper copy of the letter of recommendation (she was old-school), which I had to scan into my computer documents to upload it. It was every bit as endorsing as she promised, and I wasn't sure whether it was because the job in question was at Rocky or if she'd say such positive things regardless.

She'd written about how I'd navigated a "serious incident" and "traumatic aftermath" with law officials, students, and the school community. She'd written about how tough I'd been in the face of adversity, how I'd be a valuable attribute to any school.

I had no idea she'd thought highly of me. Her verbal feedback had always been more constructive criticism. She was right: This letter would look great in my portfolio. I just wondered if it had been worth it, going through that just to get this stellar recommendation.

I had been looking at a job out east somewhere I'd never heard of when Lucie walked in the front door. I had set myself up in the kitchen, for a change of scenery, and hadn't expected her to come home. She rarely seemed to be home anymore. She was taking her jacket off and hanging it up while she said, "Hey, I'm just here to change before I head out to a demonstration. These mother-fucking Big Bend cops are infringing on our rights again."

Her angry tone caught me off guard and stopped me in my tracks.

"What are you talking about?" I asked, concerned.

"Well, you know, since that person was murdered at your school, people have been trying to get the state supreme court involved to revoke the verdict that it was justified. The cop shot them, and still it's ruled self-defense."

She hadn't looked at me once, but if she had, she would have seen me fall into shock. I hadn't realized she'd even been aware of what was happening out in Whiteacre, let alone that she was getting involved herself. I hadn't said anything when she went on, "A bunch of us are going to demonstrate outside the district police station. We're going to let those bastards know that they can't infringe on our right to assemble, or our freedom of speech. It's one thing to rule the case as self-defense but another thing entirely to stop the people from protesting."

I took a beat of silence. How could she be so indignant about this when she wasn't even involved? When she didn't even realize how this affected the *children* in the place the people were protesting? I didn't usually get angry, but my blood was boiling. She opened her mouth to say something else, but I jumped in. "Lucie, I really don't think you should be involved in things that you don't know about. That's my opinion," I said through gritted teeth.

"I do know about it! And how can you refuse to speak up about these injustices when you are right there witnessing it? That's flat-out cowardly, Rachel. You're being part of the problem in our society. If you weren't so mousy, maybe people would listen to you more."

"I'm part of the problem? Do you even know how badly this has all affected me? How torn apart I've felt every day since all of this happened? How the sight of these people raising their voices about—"

"I do know how it's affected you!" She cut me off. "I've watched you struggle and wondered if you were going to do something about it!"

There was silence.

When I spoke again, my voice was low. "You knew I was struggling?"

Her voice was quieter. "Well . . . yeah. Anyone could see how low you felt."

"You never said anything," I said. It wasn't a question.

"I decided it'd be best to just leave you alone and let you sort it out. I mean, nothing I would say would probably help. Just like now—"

"You watched me struggle for months, feeling the worst I've felt in my life. You saw me struggling, and you chose to do nothing?" My eyes were brimmed with tears. She only nodded, her eyes wide.

I was numb. Completely and totally numb. I had nothing left to say. Nothing left to give.

Here I was, thinking she was just too self-involved to know how badly I needed someone, and she was actively making the decision to leave me alone to deal with it myself.

I had never felt so betrayed. The apartment felt too small. The room closed in around me. I had to get out.

I stood up from the table slowly, grabbing my keys and phone, not even looking at Lucie, and I walked out the door. I didn't slam it. I closed it softly but didn't lock it behind me. Lucie always made a huge deal about feeling safe in her space. Maybe she needed to know what it felt like to feel unsafe. The way I felt every day.

Out of the corner of my eye, I saw her face watching through the window as I headed down the alley.

At first, I was just walking. I had no place in mind. No tears escaped my eyes; no sobs escaped my lips. I just walked. Until I realized I was walking toward Luke's. I didn't even call. I just knocked on his door.

I was pleased that he came to the door, instead of one of his roommates, none of whom I'd even met yet, officially.

He was surprised to see me, and even more surprised to see me cry. The second I saw him, I stepped through the door to embrace him as the tears fell from my eyes. I wasn't racked with sobs, but I definitely couldn't stop the silent tears from falling.

He looked entirely confused but wrapped his arms around me anyway. After a moment, he guided me back toward his bedroom.

Later—it could have been two minutes or thirty minutes—I had calmed down enough to talk. I was sitting on his bed, leaning up against the wall while he sat toward the edge of the bed, watching me.

"So, what's going on? Rough day at middle school?" he asked, a hint of a smile on his lips. Trust him to try to lighten the mood when I was devastated.

"Always." I smirked back through my tears. "But I had a fight with my roommate, and she said some things that made me feel like shit. I just feel like shit in general," I said, looking down at my hands in my lap.

"Like what? Classic roommate stuff? You never clean up your dishes, blah blah blah? She's gotta get that you're in this really advanced program, and it takes most of your time, and you can't be the one doing housework..."

"No, that's not it," I cut him off. I usually reserved this kind of thing, but I was gushing now. "I've been going through the hardest time of my life, and she's stood by and done nothing. She has no idea how complicated and shitty this whole thing has been in the aftermath of the police shooting at my school, and now she wants me to use it for her political agenda."

The tears were still streaming down my face, but I worked to keep my voice steady.

"She said I'm too mousy for anyone to listen to me, but when I tried to speak up about what I think, she completely shut down. I just... can't stand this anymore. I can't go back there anymore. I can't comprehend working there, going back day after day. I'm so ready to be done. To go somewhere I actually want to be."

He didn't look at me. His arm was around me, but his eyes were staring at the wall. He seemed at a loss for words. I sniffed, pulling my dripping snot back into my nose.

He pulled his arm back toward him, his demeanor turning colder.

"Jeez, Rachel, I really don't know what to tell you," he said. "You really feel like all that affected you that badly?"

I nodded, growing more sheepish, and his voice turned harder.

"Do you know that people go through way worse stuff all the time? Like, imagine if you actually knew the person that died. Or if it had been a real shooting in your school. I swear, you'll take any chance to feel oppressed."

Funnily enough, I'd had the same thought about people in our program multiple times. Still, his words felt like flying arrows, stabbing deeper and deeper into my armor.

He stood up and continued, "And you know what kills me? You don't want to take that job there because you don't even have to—you can live on your damn insurance money and never need to work. You have no idea what it really means to struggle. You get that for free."

I'd never felt like I got that money for free. I felt like it was some kind of payment for losing my mother, and then my father, in a different way. I felt like it was a part of the retribution that maybe I was owed for what I'd been through. And never once had I taken it for granted or bragged about it to anyone. I had opened up to him about it, and here he was, throwing it back in my face.

I opened my mouth to argue, to say something, to stick up for myself, when he continued, clearly letting loose now, "And look at you. You're crying because someone called you mousy, and you sit here like a little girl, crying. You need to buck up if you don't want people to think that about you."

My tears stopped.

"And I'm not saying any of this to make you feel bad, so don't make me out to be an asshole. I'm just saying it to help you. You're going to have to be stronger to make it in this world. Especially in teaching."

Say something. Speak up for yourself!

But I didn't. I couldn't find it in me to form the words. I got up and walked out, and I didn't look back. If I had felt betrayed by Lucie before, I felt possibly even more so now from Luke. I'd thought that he understood what I was going through, that he picked up on all my hints about how broken I felt.

I thought he knew how much I needed his support. And maybe he did, but maybe he just didn't care. Maybe he really was just a wild card of a person—not someone you could rely on, someone with whom you never knew where you stood. Not someone dependable. Not someone worth building a future with.

I walked around the campus streets until it was dark. Without a jacket, I was cold and shivering before I decided to head back to my apartment. I was relieved to see Lucie's car was gone.

I didn't eat or shower before I got into bed. I shivered and shivered. I got back up to rifle through the bathroom drawer to find Lucie's melatonin. I'd never taken a sleep aid before, but I needed something to escape my current reality. And get some rest. So I took two, then drifted off to sleep, feeling utterly alone once more.

CHAPTER TWENTY-EIGHT

I WAS IN A kind of trance on Friday. I felt like a ghost, drifting through the morning. Though my head was afflicted and my heart felt heavy, I tried to think about anything but what was bothering me. My demeanor must have been even worse than other days because Mrs. Means picked up on it.

First thing in the morning, she was excited to tell me that they were processing my application and that I would definitely be brought in for an official interview in the next week or two. They liked to fill these positions quickly, she said.

I'd taught the first two class periods when she spoke to me in a low voice in the back of the classroom, students filing into the room and their desks, filling the room with their young human noises.

"You're not yourself today," she stated simply, looking me in my eyes, which I averted quickly.

"Yeah, I'm sorry. I have a lot on my mind. I'll perk up," I said, standing up straighter.

Her gaze turned to something else—pity? Concern, maybe?

"Let me take you out to lunch tomorrow. We can go somewhere

fabulous and talk about your future. Biagio's around noon?"

She always asked me these things without giving me any room to decline. But still, maybe it was because I wanted to avoid seeing Lucie at home, or maybe I didn't want to see Luke, or anyone else, but I nodded my acceptance just as the next class period began.

That night, I had class. It was our final course to complete our teaching license requirements. At this point, I wanted to wrap it up as soon as possible, submit my coursework, and get out of this goddamn town.

The class was run by Josephine, as one of our final requirements to get our teaching licenses. She was personally overseeing our final submissions and ensuring we kept the program statistics on the high-end of success.

When I walked into the classroom, I didn't look for Luke. I knew he was there because his presence was always known. Even though I'd planned to ignore him completely, it was impossible since I heard his voice before I even entered the room.

Why hadn't I ever noticed that he was the loudest person in the room? Most of the time, I was the quietest person. Before I may have subscribed to the belief that opposites attract, but now I wasn't so sure.

I didn't sit next to him. I didn't even sit at his table.

I sat at a table with Sarah and Briseyda at the back of the room. Class passed quietly. At my table, at least. Toward the end of class, I heard conversation coming from the table at the front, my usual table, about job applications. It'd been one of the major topics of discussion lately—who was applying where, who already had jobs lined up, who would be moving out of state, etc. I usually tried to block it out, knowing it would only make me jealous, but I was attuned when I heard my name, just like the dozens of times a day I heard my students say, "Miss H!"

This time, my name came out of Luke's mouth.

"I know Rachel's applying for jobs around here too," he was

saying, as if I wasn't ten feet away. "And her student-teaching placement is hiring, so she'll be a shoo-in for that."

"Oh, that's not even fair!" Adam said. "She's beyond lucky."

"I know, right?" Luke replied, not hiding his side glance in my direction.

My cheeks warmed and my heart thundered in my ears. I pictured myself like a wicked witch in a scary movie, a woman possessed. Unleashing my wind power, my fury, until all the windows in the room busted and the men realized their grave mistake in taunting such a powerful being.

I wasn't even mad at Luke. He'd never been anything but himself, never shown anything but his authentic colors. No, it was my fault for trusting him to be a place of solace for me. I opened myself up for him, which I rarely did. I'd poured my affections toward him, and he'd thrown them back at me. But maybe that's what I needed: to hold them for myself.

I didn't linger to see if Luke was heading to Rodeo's or if he'd try to talk to me after class. When I got home, I took a hot shower, taking time to exfoliate and moisturize my sad skin. I ate a pastry that Lucie had left on the counter, and I went to bed early, falling asleep to the sounds of old episodes of *Seinfeld*. Laugh tracks and outdated humor—maybe this was self-care.

CHAPTER TWENTY-NINE

I WORKED ALL WEEKEND. I kept my head down at my desk, my headphones blaring with loud music, and I worked my ass off getting ahead on paperwork. Only one thing pulled me out of my work mode: my Saturday lunch date.

I met Mrs. Means at the downtown restaurant in the bougie shopping village I never would have stepped into without someone like her accompanying me. Frankly, I could never afford a place like this. I was already planning to order the cheapest entrée on the menu and a water to drink.

I'd dressed my best: a linen dress that was too short to wear to school but too formal to wear to a casual college hangout. It was a cream-colored button-down dress with a collar and short sleeves. I wore it with sandals with a little heel.

I'd planned to wear this dress to graduation. If I even went. Graduation was in two weeks. I had only two weeks left of classes and student teaching. I was practically counting down the days. And with recent events, I wasn't sure if it was even worth showing up. *Or should I just go down to the registrar's office to collect my diploma and then pack up my apartment?* I had to be out one week after graduation. Which meant I needed to find a job and a place to move to, like, yesterday.

I was pleased to see that Mrs. Means (*or should I call her Isabella if we're having lunch together?*) also dressed nicely but not too formal in a sleeveless chiffon dress. It truly was a lovely day, weather-wise. It was that time in late spring where it was clear every day but not yet too hot. The flowers were fully bloomed, but allergies were no longer flaring up.

We were seated at a lovely outdoor table on the patio, with a gazebo overhead. The only people eating around us spoke in hushed tones over their glasses of red wine, dressed in clothes I could likely never afford. Or I would spill the red wine all over it and ruin it.

I didn't particularly feel like I fit in here, but I wasn't too self-conscious. Especially with Mrs. Means here, who was clearly comfortable and in her element.

The waiter came to take our drink orders before we even began talking. I was about to order water when Mrs. Means said, "Let's have something nice to celebrate you almost being done with your year. Two mimosas, please," she said to the waiter. He looked at me incredulously, like he was about to ask to see my ID, but something in Mrs. Means's shrewd look told him not to bother. He took the hint and bowed out to get the drinks.

"So," Mrs. Means began, "almost done with school. Graduation's in a couple weeks?"

"Two weeks from tomorrow," I said. A mid-Sunday afternoon graduation ceremony for the education program on the quad.

"You excited?" She looked over her sunglasses at me.

"Yeah, I mean I'm ready to be done. I'm ready for a change. I don't want to be a college student anymore; I want a career. I want to have my own classroom and my own space," I said, hoping she wouldn't take it personally. It was, but still.

"It'll be a game changer for you, I promise. Have you applied for many jobs?" She seemed genuinely curious.

I had thought maybe she'd offered to take me to lunch to end our year together, or to coach me for the interview so I'd nail it, but she was asking me in a way that made me feel like she had a real stake in what I did with my future.

"I've applied to a few. Mostly here in the valley, but also a couple farther away. Rocky is the only one in this direct area that I've seen open. I know it'd be a huge opportunity, but I'm not one-hundred-percent sure it's right for me." I might as well be honest. "How'd you decide on working there?"

She seemed to consider for a moment, right as the waiter came back with our mimosas. Before drinking, she raised her glass to me in a cheers. We clinked glasses and both sipped before she answered, "Well. It came down to a few things. Sometimes it's about where you want to be. I wanted to live in Big Bend. There's culture here. There's restaurants and music and events. I needed that. I'm not sure whether or not you need that kind of thing?"

I twisted my lips. "I like it. I just think I could use a change of scenery. But still, there are things I might stay here for . . ."

"Ah, that's the other thing," she said with a knowing smile. "I wanted to live here because of a man. I met Rick in college, and I was pretty much willing to go where he was, wherever that was. Is there someone in your life that's going to impact choices for you?"

She'd hit the nail on the head so impeccably—and I wondered if she knew it. Maybe she read me better than I thought, or maybe she was just all too aware of the influences on the decisions of a young woman.

"Well. Yes and no," I said, huffing a small laugh. "There is someone here that I thought I could have a future with. I'm not sure anymore. But I know that if I move, I'll be completely starting over. I'm kind of caught between the potential of a life here, maybe with him, and the potential of a new start someplace else. It's a lot to gamble on a job position, I know, but it is in the back of my mind a bit."

And indeed, it was. Though I was upset with Luke, and we hadn't talked since I left his house the other night, a potential life with him was still in my thoughts. It was fading, like a dream just out of reach, like I'd woken up too soon and the memory faded. But I still wanted it. Damn, I hated myself for it, but it was still the life I always wanted.

It felt weird to discuss this with Mrs. Means. With anyone. But she received it surprisingly well.

"I think it really depends on how much you're willing to gamble on this man. Does the potential justify not letting yourself experience something new? Do you really think he's the one for you?"

I know she didn't know Luke, but it was funny that she was talking like she did. Anyone who knew him might act the same way—Luke, self-referred to as the wild card. Who knew what to expect from him? I knew I shouldn't place any of my future in his hands, but it wasn't something I could just think away. He was stuck on my heart like glue. Or a parasite.

I raised my eyebrows and looked into the distance rather than at Mrs. Means as I answered her. "I think we could be really happy together. I can really see it. I'm not naive enough to let my future depend on anyone, let alone him."

She smiled. "That's what I like about you."

I smiled in return, not broadly or showing my teeth, but appreciatively. She went on.

"You're going to do great things, Rachel. I'd hate to see you waste your potential on a dream created by some man. I've seen a lot of great qualities in you this year—both as a teacher and as a person. You've got a lot going for you. Don't sell yourself short."

It was the most meaningful thing she had ever said to me.

"Thank you," I said earnestly.

"But, you know," she continued after a sip of her drink that reminded me to sip at mine, "there are other ways you could waste your potential too. Things to look out for. Places to avoid."

"What places do you think would be a waste for me?" I was genuinely curious, taking mental notes. No one had ever given me this kind of advice, this kind of guidance. I'd absorb as much as I could.

"Places that are too rural. Too far outside the cities. Isn't your hometown like that? A waste of space?"

I always felt a little protective of my hometown—it was okay when I said negative things about it, but when people who had never lived or visited there had comments, it rubbed me the wrong way. She had some kind of point, though.

"I came from a smaller town, I moved to this bigger one, so I might be ready for another change of pace. And something quieter," I said carefully.

"There's definitely something to be said for quieter. I just think you wouldn't be as happy outside of the urban neighborhoods that a city like Big Bend offers. Especially if you moved away from the campus and into a nicer neighborhood. I'd hate for you to go too far away."

She seemed like her argument was done. I didn't want to tell her that I would likely never be able to afford to live in a neighborhood like hers, one that made living in a city like this feel like a quiet, safe community.

I sipped at my drink slowly, taking in the alcohol bit by bit with my lunch so I didn't get sick like before. By the end of the meal, I didn't feel any buzz at all. I felt almost peaceful.

We debated aspects of the ancient cultures in our curriculum, talked about dream travel destinations, and gossiped about coworkers at Rocky, and she coached me for my potential interview, emphasizing repeatedly how much she'd enjoy having me as a colleague.

It was the best social interaction I had had in months. By the end, I was disappointed to go back home, back to my usual lifestyle. I was definitely ready for a change of pace in my life.

CHAPTER THIRTY

I SUBMITTED THE LAST of my coursework and my application for my teaching license on Monday. It wasn't due until the last day of classes, so I was well ahead of the game, but I couldn't wait.

I'd completed it all over the weekend. I'd had the components of it all for a while, but I just had to put them all together. It was amazing what you could accomplish when you weren't being distracted by boys fucking with your heart.

I hadn't talked to Luke all weekend. Nor had I talked to Lucie. In fact, my phone hadn't rung at all the entire weekend, but I didn't even notice. I'd been busy planning for my future, sparked by Isabella after our lunch meeting.

I'd applied to six jobs. Most of them were farther out of town, with one being in a town I hadn't even heard of before, but a couple were still in the area. And I was still contemplating the position at Rocky. The principal had told me that I would be called this week to schedule an official interview soon. Isabella had made her case to me, and her validation made me imagine a world with supportive mentors like her watching over me.

Before I could officially call myself done with my degree, though, I had to meet with Josephine. She had to sign off on my teaching license application. I had emailed back and forth with her throughout the day and decided to meet her in her office at the education building before my class began that evening.

I'd never been in Josephine's office. Maybe if I was a clever networker, like Ivy, I would have planted myself in here on week one, making sure the director of the program had my back and knew who I was specifically.

But I didn't. Because I'd never been that person. But maybe I'd try to be that kind of person, wherever I went next.

I stood outside her office by the little waiting area. Her door was closed when I walked up, and I heard voices coming from within. She must have been meeting with someone. A few minutes later, after I'd stood around trying to stop myself from fidgeting from nervousness, her door opened and Daniel walked out. He nodded his hello to me as I stepped into the door frame.

"Knock, knock," I said by way of announcing myself.

"Rachel! Please come in," she said in that extremely calm, collected way of hers. Josephine was a cool woman. She really was. From her long, dark hair that made her look younger than I knew she was to her horn-shaped glasses, she exuded a secure confidence that I hoped to emulate as a teacher.

Her office reflected that too. She had a desk in the corner, covered in papers and sticky notes in neat stacks, but the two comfortable-looking chairs in the middle of the room, clearly a more modern seating area for meetings, stood out. It felt more relaxed than the standard principal's office style, with seating facing each other, but it was still formal.

She moved behind me. "Do you mind if I close this?" she asked, motioning to the door. I shook my head as I set down my bag. "Please, sit. Would you like some candy?" I moved to sit down in the mustard-yellow chair. It was comfortable. And warm. Clearly, she or Daniel must have been sitting here.

"Oh, no thank you," I said. I'd had trouble not choking on my own spit as it was.

"Thank you for meeting with me," she said, sitting in the royal-blue chair facing mine. "I wanted to touch base with you about a few things, following your submission of your application for your licensure."

"Yes, I hope it's okay that I submitted so early," I said, not having thought that they might have us on a strict schedule for a reason.

"Oh, no worries at all! I'm excited for you. You're the first person of this year to submit. It feels good to get that accomplished, doesn't it?"

It did. It really did. Submitting my license materials also indicated that I had completed my student-teaching hours, but I was going to continue for the next couple of weeks anyway, to finish out the year.

"Yes, it does," I said simply. She wasn't looking over paperwork or at my online submission. She was looking at me, shrewdly. Expectantly? Her head was slightly cocked, and her hands were in her lap. She was definitely one of those people who looked at you like they were waiting for you to say more, and it probably worked for her more often than not.

But today I didn't have much else to say, much else to offer. When it became clear that the silence would continue on my behalf, Josephine spoke again, after intaking a large breath. "Well, I looked over everything, of course, and you are good to go. You did a wonderful job. Your application was beautiful. I have no concerns about it being approved, and you'll know by graduation if it has been accepted. But there was another reason I wanted to talk to you today."

Oh no. Great. What else did I do? Did Luke say something about me? My palms started to sweat. When I still didn't say anything, she added, "I'm sorry."

What? I blinked.

"For what?" I asked.

"I'm sorry that we left you in your situation," she said to my surprise. "With the situation at Rocky Middle School, we should have pulled you from that position to keep you from repeating the trauma every day as you went back there. We didn't catch it until it was too late, how severely you were involved. We should have—*I* should have checked in with you sooner. I'm so sorry."

I blinked again. I had not expected anyone to be thinking about what I'd been through. I certainly didn't expect anyone to apologize for what I'd been through.

After my conversation with Luke last week, I felt like maybe I was being too dramatic and sensitive about the whole thing. But having Josephine here, the director of my entire program, giving me empathy and feeling for me? I didn't even know what to say.

Tears welled in my eyes before I could stop them.

"Thank you," I said, my chin trembling slightly. "Thank you for saying that."

"If you survived this year, in the Whiteacre school district, after all that? There is nothing in your career that can stop you. You are the most resilient educator in our program."

I was a little tired of hearing how resilient this had made me, how resilient I'd been in my life. What if I didn't want to be resilient? What if I just wanted to live a calm, peaceful life?

Still, I left Josephine's office feeling better in my heart than I had in a long time.

***

Class passed quickly. Now that I had my work completed, I didn't have to worry too much, and I didn't have to pay close attention.

I did, however, eavesdrop and watch Luke from the corner of

my eye. I still didn't sit with him. I sat at a table with Sarah and the rest of the English department. That is, until we were told to sit with our own content groups. So, I had to sit with the guys. And Ivy.

I didn't want to make things tense. I wanted to be calm and casual. And I actually felt calm. For the first time maybe ever, I felt like I didn't care what anyone thought of me here. Maybe it was just because we were so close to the end of this program that I was emotionally done with it. I had nothing left to give, so why pretend?

We were instructed to discuss the importance of being a "culturally revitalizing instructor" within our subject area. We were going around the table giving our two cents about the topic at hand, and it was a little repetitive of everything we'd discussed this entire year. I was tired of hearing everyone's same old explanations.

I knew where everyone stood on basically every issue. We'd all been trained to regurgitate the same responses to these questions.

Everyone went around, and I was barely listening, until we got to Luke. I didn't want to care about his answer, but he also seemed like he was in an uppity mood. We hadn't spoken still, and I wasn't sure if he had anything to say to me. Maybe I had bruised his ego by walking out the other day. But then again, who cares?

To our group, he said, "Being culturally revitalizing means you've got to accept all people's specific needs but also know how you can call them out to make them better. Like, some girls especially can be so whiny about what they've been through and then cut you off the minute you call them out."

There were a few uncomfortable glances around the table, a few awkward smiles, like they weren't sure if they should laugh or not. *Is he joking?* I'd never known Luke to be passive aggressive, but I was fed up with his attitude. Even though no one could know that he was talking about me, with the way he'd hidden our relationship away from everyone, I'd handled the way he spoke to me in private with grace. I would *not* be spoken about like this in front of my peers. Not anymore.

"Yeah, and some people wouldn't know how to use their tiny little penis if they took a whole college course on it," I retorted. "So fuck off."

Adam's mouth hung open. Luke turned pink. Ivy snorted quietly. I was almost worried she would have "called me in" for body-shaming, but then again, she knew I was right.

It was a cheap shot, and it was a little childish, sure, but it felt good as hell.

CHAPTER THIRTY-ONE

I GOT AN INTERVIEW at Rocky. Of course, I knew I would, but it felt weird to be in such an official, formal capacity in the school when I'd been running around here for months, escorting pants-peeing students to and from the office.

It was scheduled for my last Monday workday. I felt a lot of pressure to do well, like everyone at Rocky expected me to have the job, despite there being other candidates, many of whom were possibly better qualified.

I imagined a huge rock falling on my shoulders, like I was trying to hold it up over my head, but my arms were shaking. And everyone around me was cheering for me without realizing how close I was to letting it crush me. Still, it felt good to be cheered on.

The students at Rocky were in a slightly better place. Charles hadn't wet himself in a couple of weeks now, and he was able to stay in class for almost the duration of every class period without Isabella kicking him out.

The other students were seeming like kids again too. They were more talkative in class, and not in the way they were at the beginning of the year—I didn't hear as many awful words and slurs. Not that they were kind, but still. We'd gotten into a groove, albeit a boring one, but a routine of classwork. We were almost done.

As I drove home one day that penultimate week, I thought some more about the potential of staying at Rocky, staying in Big Bend. Instead of hitting the highway and going directly home, I took a detour.

I went up and down the side streets in the Whiteacre zoning area. I drove through the neighborhoods near Rocky slowly, surveying houses and trying to imagine myself in one of them. I looked at the parks, the sidewalks, the people crossing the streets. Could I make a life here?

I pictured myself renting a small house with a little yard, where I could adopt a cat or a small dog. I imagined a simple life for myself, where I tended to my small house and kept myself busy with crafting hobbies. Where I saved my money to travel to all the places I taught about, and I had a home to go to for Thanksgiving. People who cared about me and wanted the best for me. Friends to confide in and to pick me up when I was down. I could see that life here, but it still felt incomplete somehow.

Maybe it was because that life didn't seem to be waiting for me in Big Bend.

I'd daydreamed most of the way home, so I didn't even notice that Lucie's car was home when I pulled in. We still hadn't had a full conversation since our blowup, so my stomach flipped with nerves when I opened the front door and found her standing in the kitchen.

"Hey," she began, looking at me with concern.

I took a big breath through my nose. "Hi," I said quietly.

"How are you?" she asked without moving.

"You know, I'm okay," I said, surprised at how genuinely I meant it. I hadn't been okay for a while now, but I was starting to feel more like it every day.

"I was about to make something to eat. Do you want some?"

I looked at her skeptically as I made my way into the kitchen and set my bag down. "What are you making?" Lucie was a notoriously bad cook. Or, rather, she cooked so rarely that she'd never gotten good. She basically survived on potato chips and restaurant food.

"Probably just mac and cheese. I'll make a bunch so you can eat some. You have gotten too thin, you know," she said with a raised eyebrow.

"I know," I said. "Maybe when I have my degree, I'll make more time to eat," I said, smirking down at my hands on the table.

"Yeah, I know you've been busy," she said as she got out a pot to boil the noodles, "but I think a lot of it is probably stress too. With everything this year."

I contemplated that. "Yeah, you're probably right. I know I should take better care of myself. But easier said than done, you know?"

We chatted while she cooked, and it felt really good to not have to rush off to class or work on homework all evening. Maybe my life would be less stressful now. Maybe I would make more time to take care of myself. She served up two bowls of Kraft mac and cheese when she paused, seeming to mull over the best way to say whatever she was thinking.

"You know, Rach, someone can love you and care about you so much and still have no idea how to be there for you in the way that you need," she said gently as she sat down beside me.

I was quiet for a moment. I knew she was being as heartfelt as she could be.

"I know that. I just wish you would have talked to me about it," I said. "I needed you."

"I'm sorry," Lucie said earnestly.

I knew she wouldn't change her stubborn ways, and I knew it left a permanent scar on our relationship, but having her say those words to me made me feel like we could at least heal from the argument. In time. Just like I'd heal from everything.

"You should definitely consider therapy, you know?" Lucie said as I cleaned the dishes.

I smiled. "Yeah, I've heard that before. Maybe once I get settled into a job somewhere. Speaking of, we've got to be out of this place in two weeks. What's your plan?"

She huffed a large sigh. "Well . . . Amy has another year, so I'm thinking I'm going to stick around close. I think we're going to move in together."

I don't know why I was surprised—Amy and Lucie had been together for more than a year now, and they spent almost every night together. It only occurred to me then that the only reason Lucie didn't approach the idea of moving in with her sooner was because of me. I felt a tinge of guilt, but also my heart warmed.

"I think that'd be amazing. Do you have a place yet?"

"No, we're going to look at a couple this weekend. And then you and I have got to get packing." She chuckled and slung her arm over my shoulders. The warmth felt nice.

"It's been a great few years living together," I said, suddenly feeling sentimental.

"Indeed it has," she said. "Now let's talk about sorting out our kitchen stuff."

And so we did. We packed all weekend, everything but the essentials, so that the following week could be nothing but graduation excitement.

It was the end of an era, but it was a welcome one.

***

On Monday morning I had my interview. In fact, I had multiple interviews on Monday. I had talked to Josephine and told her that I wouldn't make it to class that evening because I had two interviews on Zoom, and I didn't know how long they would go. It was all fine, of course, since I was already awaiting acceptance on my teaching license.

While we were packing, I'd had Lucie drill me with job-interview-style questions so I could prepare. I felt solid about my answers as far as my experience and work ethic could go, but I had no idea what else they might ask me. I'd interviewed for small jobs before, like customer service and retail, but never for something like this.

Rocky had interviews lined up all morning, sneaking me in at the beginning of third period. I taught the first couple of class periods before it was time, so I didn't have much time to be nervous. As I walked down the hall to the office, though, my hands started shaking.

The hardest part was convincing myself that I wanted the job. In the back of my mind, I thought it would be a relief if someone else was better qualified and they were forced to pick them over me. At least that way I wouldn't be letting them down; they'd be letting me down. And I was used to being let down.

I swung open the door to the main office, trying not to think about the body camera footage of Ron escorting Sammie out this door. I was so distracted by the thought that I didn't even register who was sitting in the waiting chairs.

"Hey, Rachel," Daniel said as he waved. He was seated next to another guy who was bald but had a beard, and there was a woman in her late thirties sitting across from them both. All here for the interview.

My stomach dropped. *This is what you wanted*, I tried to remind myself. If one of them got the job, I'd be off the hook.

Except I had no other real leads, except my Zoom interviews later. As someone who liked to plan ahead, I was not good at this whole "you'll be out on your ass in less than two weeks, but you'll definitely get it figured out by then" thing. I wasn't a wild card like Luke. I needed structure.

Still, I smiled at Daniel. He'd always been so nice to me, and I knew he was a genuinely good person.

"Here to compete for a job, huh?" I said, knowing it'd diffuse some of the tension in the room. It was always weird to be in such a competitive job market, sharing a space together before the interviews.

Daniel was about to say something else when Mrs. Cairns stuck her head out of her office and said, "Rachel, we're ready for you now."

I nodded at her and followed. She walked past her office, into the empty conference room behind her, the one where I had the most awkward massage of my life.

Seated in the room already was the vice principal, Ryan, and an older, overweight woman I didn't know—someone in Human Resources?

I took a seat at the head of the table and felt their eyes on me.

"So, Rachel," Cairns began. "You've been a valuable asset to our school this year. I know we'd love to have you stay on, and the kids would certainly love to have you stick around. What we're going to do is round-robin some questions for you, and you'll just tell us whatever comes to mind, okay?"

"Sounds great." I smiled and put on my nicest voice.

"And then," Ryan said, "we've got some other people to interview, like you saw, and if you make it past this first round of interviews, then we'll call you back next week for another round. I know school ends this week, but you'll still be around, right?"

I was a little appalled. Multiple rounds of interviews at this shitty middle school? Where they already knew me? I was offended, if I'm being honest. But I knew these jobs were coveted, police shooting or not.

"Yes, I should be around next week. I graduate next Sunday, and then I'll quickly need to make plans for what happens next."

That seemed to satisfy all three of them.

"So, Rachel, why are you in education? Why spend your day with adolescents?"

An easy question, really. I started into my spiel about how I became a teacher because I care about education as a source of power, and all students can have that power regardless of the circumstances of their lives, and I want to be the person I didn't have when I was younger. I meant every word, and they seemed intrigued, nodding, but I wasn't thinking about what I was saying.

I was thinking about how much I actually didn't want to work there.

I was thinking about how staying at Rocky, where I had this extremely rough year, would feel like being stuck in place.

I was thinking about Josephine's words—how they should have pulled me from here so I wouldn't have to keep coming back to the place I experienced the worst day of my life.

I thought about the dynamic with Isabella Means, how she'd always be a mentor to me rather than an equal colleague if we worked together.

I was thinking about Daniel and the other applicants waiting in the office, whose nervous smiles made it clear that they wanted to be here.

I thought about how they'd push us through to another round of interviews, where I'd have to fight even harder for a job I didn't even really want, deep down in my heart.

Could I be appreciative of the opportunity of student teaching here, grateful for the interview experience, and still want to move on? Did that make me a bad person?

They continued asking questions while I contemplated all of this. I answered politely, and they nodded and smiled, and I knew I'd get through to the second round. I might even get the job.

But deep down, I knew what I had to do.

CHAPTER THIRTY-TWO

MY LAST TWO days at Rocky were bittersweet. I expected them to only be bitter, as middle school students get a little extra wild right before summer break hits.

It was weird, though—the students were sentimental. I was getting hugs. I was getting sweet notes and cards. I hadn't seen this behavior all year—mostly, they just heckled me and told me they didn't like my outfits. And though I was ready to leave, I knew I would miss these kids who had made such a huge impact on me. I already knew that years down the line, even after I'd taught hundreds of students, these faces would be imprinted in my mind forever. My first students.

That was something I really liked about teaching—tying up loose ends. I liked that when one year ended, all things came together and wrapped up. Then you got a break before starting it all over again the next year. I liked the cycle of it all.

I was actually going to miss some of the students. Definitely not all, but I was going to be sad not to see them grow up more. There had already been such a difference over the year. Now they were closer to being eighth graders than sixth graders, and the change was monumental.

Isabella gave me a nice card with a gift card to Staples, telling me to buy some essentials for my own classroom. I appreciated the gesture more than she knew. She even gave me a small hug and told me to call her if I needed advice or help, wherever I ended up.

In all, it was a nice end to my year of student teaching. After our end-of-year assembly, I waved goodbye with the other teachers as the school buses drove away; then I made to leave.

I opened my car door but stopped myself from getting in. I turned and looked back at Rocky one more time.

The early summer breeze was blowing my hair softly, and I looked up at the clear blue sky. It was a beautiful day. I thought about the days I spent there, rolling up in the morning with so much dread turning in my stomach that I felt sick.

It really didn't look so bad on the outside. But I couldn't shake the picture of Sammie's body under the tarp or Officer Ron's face the day he came back—gaunt, hollow, and somehow changed from the person he was before.

I hoped that everyone there found peace.

I took one last breath of the clear air. I shut my car door, and I drove away from Rocky Middle School. Permanently.

***

I liked that all aspects of my life were wrapping up and starting fresh.

Our apartment was almost entirely packed up, to the point that we had to eat takeout because our cookware was in boxes. Lucie and Amy had secured a lease on a new apartment on the south side of campus, and I was helping them move most of the stuff over the weekend, in between the graduation hubbub.

That's what Saturday consisted of: packing, parties, packages.

A knock at the door while I was getting ready to make the rounds at various graduation parties turned out to be a delivery from my grandma. She'd sent a gift basket with teachery items like pens and a cute stapler, a mug, and some graduation goods from her and some of her friends down in Arizona.

I called Grandma to thank her, updating her on all my latest plans and promising to make the trip down to Tucson soon, and then I headed out to the graduation parties. I had tagged along with Lucie to her friends' places, and now I was going to some of the cohorts' places. Starting with Adam.

Adam's party was at a restaurant downtown—his parents had gone all out to celebrate his graduation.

Everyone from our cohort seemed to be there when I walked in—even Josephine made an appearance. Adam had gotten on her good side early. In fact, he was on everyone's good side, it seemed.

People were eating hors d'oeuvres and standing around with beers in their hands. I made conversation with Adam's girlfriend, Haley, and congratulated Briseyda and Jack, both of whom had secured jobs nearby, and I tried to enjoy the chance to mingle with the people that I would probably never see again.

And if Luke was there, I didn't even notice.

***

Graduation day came at last. We were on the lawn outside the education building, where they'd set up a small stage and hundreds of chairs. It felt good to wear the ridiculous hat and walk across the stage. No one in my family had ever graduated from college, and it felt like a big accomplishment.

So we walked across the stage, one by one, as they called out our names. We all cheered for each other, bonded by the most stressful year of school any of us had ever had. I was excited to see where they all ended up.

After we moved our tassels to the left side, they announced that we were all graduates, and then they played an upbeat song while everyone cheered.

We hugged, mingled, and wished each other well. I was ready to begin my walk home when Sarah caught me.

"Hey, Rachel! What are you doing now? My parents were wondering if you and your family wanted to join us for dinner," she said.

The two people behind her must have been her parents. They were exuding warmth, with broad smiles on their faces. Sarah looked so much like both of them—her mom had honey-blond hair and perfectly straight teeth; her dad had a beard that was peppered with gray and cut close to his face, but his eyes were exactly like Sarah's. They looked at me expectantly.

"I don't have any family here. It's just me," I said, trying not to sound sad about it.

"Oh, then we insist," Sarah's dad said. "Please join us! We'd love to treat you girls."

"That sounds great, actually," I said as they began to turn toward the parking lot, which had effectively turned into a zoo of traffic.

I followed closely behind Sarah and her family when someone tapped my shoulder. My stomach was in knots as I turned around. I had expected to see Luke, whose parents had sat with Amber, the bitchy girl from Luke's birthday party. I had smiled at them during graduation but didn't engage otherwise. I had come to my own terms about how things ended between us, without closure. *Sometimes things don't get wrapped up nicely. They just hurt for a while.*

But when I turned around, it wasn't Luke. It was Daniel. He had a broad smile.

"I made it to the second round at Rocky Middle! Did you?"

I only debated my answer for a moment. I plastered a sheepish smile on my face.

"No, no, I didn't. Congratulations, though! I hope you get it!"

He looked conflicted. I could see the surprise cross his face, mixed with the excitement and pride, but also concern, like maybe he'd said the wrong thing and hurt my feelings. He certainly didn't want to make anyone uncomfortable.

"Damn, really?" He was talking loudly over the crowd of people. "I would have thought you did. I'm sorry. Are you bummed?"

I smiled. "No, I have other plans lined up. I was just offered a job out in Hartsville, and I'm looking for an apartment to rent. Good luck, though, Daniel, and let me know if you get it! You have my number, right?"

He assured me that he did, and with that, I walked away, meeting Sarah where she'd waited for me.

I could have told Daniel the whole truth. I could have told him that I actually had been offered a second interview, but that I'd turned it down. That I'd spoken his name in a positive way during my first interview to try to get it in their heads. That I had made my choice to leave.

I could have told him, but sometimes ignorance is bliss. Innocence is bliss.

EPILOGUE

Five Years Later

SOME JUNIOR BOYS were arguing about something that happened in math class; I was trying not to listen, but when they talk so loudly, it's hardly considered eavesdropping. I stared at my computer, not really comprehending the email I was reading.

"Bruh, she totally ripped Avant a new one!" one of them said, hardly containing his laughter. Teenage boys got a kick out of making fun of each other. Sometimes it wasn't clear to me when to intervene or when they were just being silly.

It's hard to gauge the emotions of people who try to hide them, which gets complicated when your job is to make sure no one is being unkind.

"Dude, what did she say again?" said another student, who obviously wasn't there for the original event and wanted a play-by-play.

"So, we were playing baseball with the tape ball we made, and Avant swung so hard! The ball hit the whiteboard right next to Mrs.

Garcia, and she blew up at him," he said with a smile. "She told Avant he needed to grow up or get out of her classroom."

They erupted in laughter. All except Avant, who didn't quite look like he thought the whole thing was humorous. Now was my time to intervene, especially since the rest of the class had stopped working to listen to the story.

"Guys," I said as I wheeled away from my computer, looking over at them, "Are we getting any work done, or are we just roasting Avant?"

They erupted in laughter again, this time Avant joining in. He was a good kid, and I knew my attention would perk him up.

"Mrs. Thomas," Avant asked me, "do you think I need to grow up?"

The rest of the boys, and the class, for that matter, awaited my response.

I took a deep breath and pulled my glasses off my face. "Well, Avant, I don't really believe in telling students to grow up. I believe in letting kids enjoy the innocence of childhood as long as they can. But you really shouldn't be throwing things in Mrs. Garcia's class."

That seemed to satisfy all of them as they finally got to work on their assignment. Avant caught my eye and gave me a soft, appreciative smile. At that moment, Charles's face flashed through my mind.

ACKNOWLEDGMENTS

Writing *Gray Area* was a therapeutic experience for me, and I wasn't sure if it was something I would be brave enough to publish. Like Rachel, I tend to keep things close to my chest. Thank you to everyone who has encouraged me to pursue this novel.

To Gaven, my husband and my rock, thank you for loving me the way I need to be loved and supporting me as I pursue all of my endeavors. You've never once dampened my dreams, and I love you so much.

To my mommy, Lori, for being my first reader and supporter: thank you for passing on the joy of reading. To the rest of my family and friends, thank you for being the support system that has gotten me through all of life's challenges.

To the team at Koehler Books who took a chance on an unknown author, guided me through the publishing process without ever being condescending, and making an okay manuscript into a decent book, thank you for your guidance and support.

To every colleague I've had in my teaching career, and my former cohort members from UOTeach, thank you for what you do, and this book is for you.

To my two cooperating teachers who guided me through my

own student-teaching experience, Elizabeth Fine and Matthew Ciaffoni, thank you for being leagues better than the mentors in *Gray Area*. My experiences in your classrooms were invaluable, and I cherish those memories of how I learned to teach.

Last, to every student I've ever had: I love you, and I'm proud of you. Thank you for making my teaching career all that it is, lighting my life with joy, teaching me new slang, and sharing a love of learning with me.

www.ingramcontent.com/pod-product-compliance
Lightning Source LLC
LaVergne TN
LVHW041929070526
838199LV00051BA/2761